RUPTURES INTO SILENCE

Carol Andrews Redhead

Order this book online at www.trafford.com
or email orders@trafford.com

Most Trafford titles are also available at major online book retailers.

Note for Librarians: A cataloguing record for this book is available from Library
and Archives Canada at www.collectionscanada.ca/amicus/index-e.html

Printed in Victoria, BC, Canada.

ISBN: 978-1-4269-1837-7 (sc)
ISBN: 978-1-4269-1838-4 (dj)

Library of Congress Control Number: 2009936879

*Our mission is to efficiently provide the world's finest, most comprehensive book publishing
service, enabling every author to experience success. To find out how to publish your
book, your way, and have it available worldwide, visit us online at www.trafford.com*

Trafford rev. 10/20/09

 www.trafford.com

North America & international
toll-free: 1 888 232 4444 (USA & Canada)
phone: 250 383 6864 ♦ fax: 812 355 4082

For my father, Laurie ...

May the blessing of the rain be on you—
the soft sweet rain.
May it fall upon your spirit
so that all the little flowers may spring up,
and shed their sweetness on the air.
May the blessing of the great rains be on you,
may they beat upon your spirit
and wash it fair and clean,
and leave there many a shining pool
where the blue of heaven shines,
and sometimes a star.

May the good earth be soft under you
when you rest upon it,
and may it rest easy over you when,
at the last, you lay out under it,
And may it rest so lightly over you
that your soul may be out
from under it quickly,
and up, and off,
And be on its way to God

Irish Blessing

RUPTURES
INTO
SILENCE

PREFACE

I always wanted to write. Ideas were always floating around in my head. Sometimes I will 'write' a paragraph in my head and sometimes I would 'write' what I would think of as a chapter – dialogue and all. Of course when I was much, much younger I had neither the wisdom nor the common sense to put all these myriad ideas on paper. But, as I got older I wrote many short stories which I kept to myself because I was self-conscious of what people would think about them. Stories, as many of you may know sometimes write themselves and sometimes they say more about you than you think – at least so many of my friends tell me. I do believe though, that stories are wonderful creations that sometimes pop out of your head like pink, bubbly chewing gum out of the mouth of a child. And sometimes they are well thought out; slowly developing pieces of work which the writer painstakingly and conscientiously organize into interesting prose or poetry.

***

When I began to teach Language and Literature at Secondary School and later when I became a Guidance Officer in these same schools, I realized that much of the Literature that I like to write – and read – was similar to that which young people expressed as being interesting to them. Young people want to read about themselves, to see images of themselves on the page, by means of those squiggly wonderful black marks that we call words. Through ideas, opinions and feelings expressed in these words; through phrases, sentences, paragraphs and chapters - through books - they can relate to circumstances that explain and clarify those issues that acutely interest them. In other words, I realised that students wanted to read about issues that affected them intimately and which would help them comprehend the predicament of present day youth. Thus, I recognised that what these young people wanted was information about matters of which I can write: They desired to understand themselves better; to know more about relationships, to feel comfortable in their sexuality, to discern through their own selves, how life can be so creative and at the same time be so destructive? In fact, young people desire to grasp the meaning of life and to claim the inevitability of death.

***

I believe that I could present these ideas in ways in which young people as well as adults can read and enjoy. Not only will it help them to understand themselves, but maybe, to some measure, if written interestingly enough, they may return to the wonder of the 'written word' - and what more can an English teacher ask?

Carol Laura Andrews-Redhead

ONE

Olivia

One of the luckiest things that can happen to you in life is,
I think, to have a happy childhood

Agatha Christie (1890-1976),

ONE

They said she was my grandmother's favorite child and I knew why Tante Margaret was the favourite. Granny had told me why, making me swear not to tell anyone. And for nearly my entire life I kept my grandmother's secret. And even though now, that I am a grown woman, I have never said a single word to anyone - not even to my Uncle Thomas who would have thought I was lying anyway. So, I kept quiet. I didn't even tell Anna, my best friend, who lived next door and who might have squealed to *her* mother.

Anna was my best friend and her mother Lucille, was my grandmother's confidante. As most people in our village, both Anna and Lucille thought we were a strange family – and we were, for most members of my family did not talk much to one another. Even our neighbours thought we were strange – even quaint people. It was not that we were quiet really, but we never did speak much to one another. We never t*alked.* Even my two uncles, who lived with us, never expressed any personal thoughts to each other. They *never* talked about the way they *felt* about things; about life, about love, about *important* matters. Silent and wary of others in our own group, our family circled one another, always looking, but averting our eyes when we were being looked at. And in a house where souls existed, but never looked, never touched, never talked, Tante Margaret was an aberration: *She talked too much* and what she said – and did - was outrageous. Her dreadful sayings were her weapon and these words were always precise and hurtful. Tante Margaret's words were daggers that always found their mark. Embittered words spewed from her spirit like an intense and rapid erupting volcano; hot, acrid, abrasive, flowing outward in a torrent of vitriol and venom. And if she, my mother's only and older sister, ever thought of any words of endearment, they remained unsaid ...

Now, grown old and frail, Tante Margaret lay paralysed in her crumpled bed. Her eyes remained half opened. I stood close to her bed and gazed down in wonder at my grandmother's favourite child and I felt afraid – again. As a young child, I had thought that Tante Margaret was "fearful', *but, also wonderful*. She had always seemed to me to be a magnificent specimen of femaleness who looked like a colossus and who had a mouth to match. Tante Margaret was now the antithesis of her former extraordinary self; she was a figure of dissipation and neglect. Her physical deterioration was uncanny. She had grown old and weak. In my consternation at the rapid physical deterioration of my aunt, I asked myself in wonder: In reality, was *this* Tante Margaret's true self; her 'real' self? Was she always a wretched woman whose vulnerability was hidden behind a façade of power? It was these conflicting images of female strength and power and now, rapid physical deterioration that re-ignited in me feelings of fear. I was overwhelmed. I thought to myself that there is really no pain like living in this frail, transitory body. I sighed. Life can be *so* cruel; *so short, so* swift and *so sure* as it irrevocably confers its death sentence.

Standing here, looking down at this figure of contradiction and conflict, I realised that there were many things that I never did comprehend about our family – especially Tante Margaret - and I believe now that, that lack of understanding originated partly from my fear of this woman. I certainly did not understand *why* I was so afraid of her, neither could I control the choking sensations of anxiety I experienced in her presence. Even as a child, I *knew* that I was angry with this woman I *knew* that those strong debilitating emotions that I experienced in her presence; fear, anger, anxiety - did not come from any form of accusation by her or her annoyance with me, but it originated from some unknown l*ocation* - a strange place that I inhabited, only in Tante's presence. It was a place where rationality did not reside; a pure emotional site that was re-presented as a deep down spiritual rejection of kin. I was ashamed of this rejection, but at the same time, I was fascinated by Tante Margaret. My mother Josephine, would have said it was a fascination with evil – a human frailty – a weakness that I needed to control. However, whenever Tante Margaret was near, this fear and a kind of excitement that I did not fully understand, pervaded my whole being, inserted itself in the depths of my soul and changed the psychological palette with which I viewed the world. This trepidation *and* wonder in the presence of my aunt, changed my perception of the world from a soothing blue, in which everything I knew and thought was calm and under control, to a fiery red, in which my world became a mix of heat and dread: Every thought became muddled and obsessive. Every action was tainted with guilt. It felt like hell.

As I pulled up the old, dusty rocking chair from behind the bed and sat gingerly on its edge, I felt the old cane digging into my thigh, and I was uncomfortable. That old chair, the same one in which Tante Margaret had always sat, rocking, back and forth, back and forth, back and forth, as she gazed out her large bedroom window at some distant place which she inhabited only in her mind, had remained vacant for the last three months. No one came to see her, to rub her legs, to comb her thick, grey hair – or to look after the needs that go beyond the mere physical. And I thought to myself, s*he has lain here for the last three months; an old misshapen body, unloved, uncared for, unvisited.*

Now, as I peered at this old woman, I became breathless. It was remarkable how Tante Margaret's once beautiful, smooth black skin had become so discolored. Loose and wrinkled, splotches of light khakhi-coloured spots were surrounded by reddish, circular blotches and these strange bruises covered her entire body. Her skin, without fat or form, fell around her thin, angular frame in clumpy folds that drooped onto the creased, unclean bed-sheet. Her skin resembled my grandfather's old, discarded, unpolished, dried out shoe that my grandmother had worn around the farm when she looked after her chickens. That shoe was battered and out of shape. The leather had begun to disintegrate; white and green with mould, grime had settled in the corner of its folds. And now grime was clearly visible in the folds of Tante Magaret's skin, making her body seem like that of an old, sick animal as it slowly and painfully collapses into a putrid mass of disintegrating cells. That beautiful long body of which she was once so proud was now, not only encrusted with dirt, but also contorted, like the old skeletal branches of a dying fruit tree. But then some would say that she *was a contortionist.* It was her words that had made her so; this woman was able to twist any story so that it suited her fancy.

For myself, Life had taught me many lessons. Was this to be another one ... That at Life's conclusion, do you have a choice; to relive the world of sensation and passion, or do you, like Tante Margaret, collapse into decay?

In an attempt to move as far away from this awful sight as possible, but at the same time to be as close to her as I could allow myself to get, I leaned forward gingerly while, simultaneously raising my body off the old rocking chair. My eyes fell on her hands. They were close fisted. Her fingernails, the ones that were visible, were long, with dirt embedded at the base of each discolored one. The irony was that those hands had not done much hard work. Always pristine, always well-manicured, her hands had been a manifestation of her assumed superiority in the village. Now, dirty and discoloured, they punctuated her rapid physical deterioration. I did not know whether it was facing that fact of decay which sat so heavily on my spirit, but seeing the incredible advancement of whatever illness engulfed her body and the resulting physical violation of that strong, powerful woman, who in life controlled all and everything around her, shocked me. I collapsed back onto the rocking chair.

I closed my eyes to remove that painful image from my consciousness. Darkness enveloped me and made me more powerfully aware, of my own body. Suddenly, I realized that I was unable to breathe. Unaware that I had held my breath for so long, I was suffocating. I could feel my whole body becoming tight, my muscles ached, the tingling in my feet moved quickly up my spine and settled uncomfortably at the back of my neck. The pain in my chest was unbearable; it seemed to pierce through to my heart. But as sick and uncomfortable as I felt in that old cluttered, musty, smelly, cold room, I could not bring myself to get off that old chair. I too, was paralysed. Fear constrained my movement. I opened my eyes and for some inexplicable reason, I felt this old woman was looking at me - just the way she did when I was young. But her eyes were closed, weren't they? To ease the tension, I shifted again uneasily in the old rocking chair and as I did so, the chair moved unexpectedly to the right. It happened so quickly, that I had to grab the dirty bedclothes to save myself from falling. As I righted myself, my hand touched her leg and her eyes seemed to fly open.

What was that?!

I knew Olivia was sitting there. I could feel her aura. She was always uncomfortable in my presence ... and I expect now she feels the same. She was a pretty child though and I guess she still is- in a soft, yielding way. But her looks got her nowhere!! Twice divorced and foolish enough to want to marry again. Why does she think that having a child will fill that emptiness within? Foolish, insipid child. Her mother was even more foolish than she is – not half as pretty though. Thank God, she left this earth early. You never can tell what transgressions she would have committed. It has always surprised me that people who do not know who they are and what they can do, can get themselves into so much trouble ....

She thinks I am asleep. But I am watching her as she watches me. ...

This must be the way God feels; peering into the lives of people when they do not know He is looking.......... I guess I am old enough, certainly sick enough, to experience feelings of omniscience - and it feels good. I like it almost better than walking around in a wholesome body.

Ironically, you cannot perceive such, unless you are in a position like me; flat on your back without the use of limbs - or tongue. I guess ... impotence is its own power.

I could feel a change in her, but I did not know what it was. I was afraid and uncomfortable. I had to do something, so I got up to relieve the discomfort that pervaded my entire body. I walked over behind the bed in order to open one of the two windows on the other side of the room. The glass in the frames was dirty and the window was stuck. I had to push hard, while at the same time being careful not to cut myself. As I pushed, the hinges on the window squeaked loudly and both sides flew open simultaneously. Black dust settled quickly on my hands. However, no air rushed in to alleviate that musty smell. No sun peeked in.

It was still outside. It had been raining heavily for a few days after a short period of drought and the musky smell of the earth had been replaced with the soggy scent of stagnant mud. As a child, I used to like to play in the mud. It was so soft, so wet!!! Now, there weren't many trees in the yard. The big old mango tree, its trunk gnarled with age and dark brown in places from the disease that infected its bark, stood bent, hovering over the roof of the house like an open-winged bat – out of place in the murky daylight. At its roots, the mud settled in small pools - as it had always done. Small dried out leaves circled in the dirty water, hitting against each other and then moving apart. Some were broken and full of holes, others just moved, going with the flow. I gazed at the small concentric whirls in the pool as the muddy water moved listlessly in the slight wind that passed through the mango tree. The leaves of the tree seemed to shiver in the same way as my body.

In the years I had been away, this mango tree had grown really huge. Strange enough, it was mango season, but there was no fruit on *this* tree – although, despite its deformed trunk, the leaves were lush, the branches extending far outwards, providing shade for the old wooden house. I had loved to climb that tree as a child. I felt safe in its branches, for it allowed me the opportunity to escape from the discomforting silences in our house. From the top of the mango tree, you could almost see forever – a big wide world in which the large houses in the valley, with their gigantic overhanging roofs were made distinctive by the wide sheets of galvanize of diverse colours, of grey and red and green. In these houses, where I had presumed people talked and joked and laughed, large windows were left wide open – all day, all night, allowing their multicolored, bright curtains the freedom to blow energetically in the breeze. As a child, on top of the world, in my leafy heaven, I imagined these giant houses filled with people, both large and small, who, talked and laughed loudly and incessantly with one another. I guess they could be happy; they did not have to keep big secrets - for *their* grandmother.

It is really strange that, as a child, I perceived everything as being large – larger than life; the trees were huge, the houses were large, my parents were big and tall and my aunt, Tante Margaret, was a monstrous figure who everyone was afraid of and out of whose mouth flowed huge words – considerable, significant and most times, offensive. So for me, the mango tree was a haven that allowed me to get away from my childish anxieties and I regretted its aging. Representing a big, wide, magnificent world beyond the mundane, this mango tree had symbolized huge possibility to me who, small and insignificant, was able to hide in its folds and to see everything from above – like God I guess.

In my family, God was the main player in our lives. At home, we were not really religious, meaning that we rarely ever went to church - except for Christmas, christenings or funerals. However, contradictorily enough, everything was left to God: "God knows best". "It is God's Will". "God is good". "Live in the fear of God". My grandmother believed these sayings and most of the words she spoke related to Him in some way or other – except for what she had told me about Tante Margaret.

As a child, I always wondered why God controlled everything and everybody. What was it about Him that could keep everyone so quiet – except Tante Margaret? Wasn't she afraid of Him? How could she be so brave? My mother was afraid of Him –so much so that she kept a picture of Him under her pillow and was always mumbling to Him at nights. She made me afraid of Him too – for a while, whilst I was very young – until I began to pay close attention to Tante Margaret. *She* was certainly more interesting. She did not appear to be afraid of anyone or anything. I wondered how she could be like that! How could she say those things she said to everyone about anything? I realized now that for me, the 'fear' my grandmother and my mother thought should be reserved for God, was transferred onto the living body of my transgressive aunt.

I remember, as if it were yesterday, seeing her walk through the forested path that led to our house on one dark rainy day. She was so tall. She wore a dark blue dress, down to her ankles. It flowed around her in folds that were really pleats, interspersed with some sort of white fabric on which there were painted big yellow flowers. She looked out of place; like a huge, colourful bat, stalking the earth in the daylight. She was wearing a huge dark blue hat that matched her dress perfectly. A broad white silk ribbon with a large bow circled the crown of her hat and flew behind her like wings. Her teeth, in the smooth dark skin of her face, did not appear to be the immaculate white I knew it to be, but it seemed to be coated with a red tinge – pinky white. She frightened me – until I realized that the bounteous red hibiscus flowers planted along the path by my grandmother were

9

being reflected on the flashing teeth of the wide smile Tante Margaret offered me. So, I was afraid of her. In her presence, my imagination ran wild. Her very aura crept into my soul and that sensation of dread made it seem as though she was sucking away at my very spirit.

Now, as an adult, gazing down at her still form I prayed that, *that* God who she decried and blasphemed, would have mercy on her soul. The words of prayer, mixed with sadness and I don't know what, broke from my lips and in a torrent of fear, so much like that of my own mother's, I mumbled her name in a whisper ....Tante Margaret. ...Tante Margaret. The words fell off my lips. The grief overwhelmed me. Fear consumed my body and I wondered if what Granny said was true ....

I wish I could speak to her. She appears in so much pain. I never truly paid any attention to why she feared me so. I guess I wasn't interested enough to find out. Actually, in my younger years I thought it was funny; so caught up in my own world of the material. But she was a foolish child! - always squirming in her seat. I always wondered why children could not sit still. Why did they have to be so ..... intrusive. Big eyes of children always frightened me. They see somewhere within the soul where the adult cannot reach...... I remember Mother saying, always, that innocence of children is to be protected at all cost. But she did not protect this child. She told her secrets that no child should have to carry... No child should be burdened with the knowledge of adults.

TWO

Because I could not stop for Death—
He kindly stopped for me—

Emily Dickinson (1830-1886)

TWO

In the village of Southwood, near the fishing village of Erin in Taringa, any death was time for celebration. Villagers believed that the spirit of the 'Dead One' returns to its place in the sky, somewhere, where such spirits are reconciled with their ancestors. Because of this belief, there were always a lot of feasting and loud prayers and chanting, mixed with the loud keening of the bereaved. And these conflicting noises - of both loud sighing and much singing – were meant to accompany the soul back to its Home.

It was on a cold night, at the wake of her father that Margaret Vivian just turned sixteen, sat on an old bench with her long, skinny legs swinging back and forth, back and forth, back and forth. Her father, Graham, had died suddenly from what some villagers thought was constant and consistent nagging from his obstreperous wife, Viola. In fact, Graham had died from a heart attack, just as his father and his father's father. Because of these early and sudden deaths in the family, the villagers had accepted the early passing of men in the Manette family as inevitable. Even Viola, Margaret Vivian's mother, showed no real regret. Consequently, none of the villagers paid much attention to the happy child, sitting near the front door, swinging her long legs back and forth, back and forth, back and forth to the rhythm of a present-day calypso.

In quiet contrast to Viola's seeming disinterest in the death of her husband and Margaret Vivian's indifference to her father's passing, Josephine, Margaret's younger sister, was huddled in a dark corner of the living room. Feeling forlorn and confused at her father's passing, she had ensconced herself behind the rocking chair, where her father had sat on evenings after work to take off his construction boots and where he read the newspapers which he usually brought from his supervisor's office. She was twelve years old, an introverted child, for whom the greatest point in her life thus far, was to run every afternoon to greet her tired father as he made his way home. His shoulders were always bent forward, his legs seeming robot-like, moved one before the other, up the steep incline and then up the wooden steps of his home until, his thin body, weary and frustrated from the long hours of hard labour on the construction site, collapsed onto his rocking chair. Graham worked on the site where they were building a new secondary school in the area. He was glad for the job, not only because the money was good, but mainly because he was happy to know that Josephine would not have to leave the village – as Margaret Vivian did - and spend weeks at his brother-in-law in town, in order to get an education.

Now, Josephine, alone and bereft, devastated at this premature passing of her beloved father and not knowing what to do, did what she knew best; she huddled at the back of his rocking chair. He would no longer be able to read to her and to spell out the 'hard' words that were written in the paper. To accommodate her large frame behind the chair (for she too, like Margaret Vivian was tall for her age) she hugged her arms around her knees and pulled her knees close to her chin. Long tears flowed down her cheeks. She did not make a sound, for she was afraid her mother would hear her. She remained as quiet as her father had been during the constant affront of abuse from his insistent wife. As she attempted to stifle the sobs that threatened to overwhelm her, her chest heaved in the same way that her father's had done as he had fought to breathe.

She was just entering the room, fresh from her bath, after having run a little further up the hill than usual to meet her father that day. Having bathe quickly before she and her father shared their precious, private time together, she was hustling into the room when she saw her father grab his chest, and without a sound, collapsed onto the floor. He seemed to be experiencing much distress; his chest moved erratically – up and down, up and down, up and down and his mouth, wide open, let out quick, short snorts that corresponded to the opening wide of his nostrils. She could not move. Her fast legs that ran with so much alacrity up the hill so many times to greet her father, now would not respond. Josephine watched in amazement as her loving father writhed in pain. She could not help him. She did not know what to do. As she watched helplessly, his legs, stretched out before him. Then, his entire body convulsed. The pages of the newspaper were scattered every way on the floor. Graham seemed to shiver, as if from extreme cold - twice - and then, he became still.

The sudden explosion of noise from Josephine's mouth escaped without volition. It startled her and the screams brought her mother hustling into the room.

"Josephine! What is the matter with you?"

Josephine pointed to the floor. Viola eyes quickly followed Josephine's finger and she saw her husband stretched out, still, on the cold, wooden floor. Her first reaction was one of annoyance. This emotion fleetingly passed across her face and was replaced, almost immediately, by worry and concern. Quickly she turned to her younger daughter;

"Go get Mrs. Brewster!"

Mrs. Fiona Brewster, her best friend's mother, was sitting in her kitchen shelling peas for lunch the next day. She was talking to her husband as he lay sprawled in an old hammock on the outer verandah. Mr. Brewster, wearing only an old, dirty vest and short khaki pants, was swinging in his hammock, back and forth, back and forth, back and forth while, at the same time, picking his teeth with a matchstick. He was laughing uproariously at some ludicrous statement his wife had just made. Mr. Brewster had had a good catch at sea that day and was pleased with himself. But then, the sudden, hysterical cries of Josephine as she climbed over the old wire fence that separated their homes immediately caught his attention. Closing his mouth suddenly from his loud laughter, he said,

"So what wrong now Josephine!!! Yuh see another snake?"

This was a standing joke between Josephine and Mr. Brewster, for when Josephine was about six years old she had spotted what looked like a snake near the water barrel and had run screaming across the fence to Mr. Brewster, since her father was not at home. The 'big snake' had turned out to be a large, long twisted twig that had acquired some greenish spots as it lay behind the water barrel.

"Something's wrong with Daddy! Ma Ma say to come!"

Mr. Brewster jumped out of his hammock and his wife, in her haste to follow him, dropped the bowl of peas she was shelling on to the floor. The little green peas rolled in every direction; under Mr. Brewster's hammock, below the step where Mrs. Brewster was sitting, out into the yard and around the body of the dog, Spirit, who stirred himself long enough to sniff disinterestedly at a few, and then return to his dream. Both Mr. and Mrs. Brewster hastened across the yard to their neighbour's house.

The house was quiet as usual. Rushing in through the kitchen, Mrs. Brewster bustled passed her husband and saw Graham lying on the floor. His body was very still. His handsome face was turned to one side and there was a thick whitish stuff at one corner of his mouth. His eyes were wide open, and he appeared to be staring way past her, over her shoulder, looking at something – or someone - behind her. Viola was stooping over him, to one side. One tie, at the end of her apron was trailing on the floor as the bow had become undone; the other end was lying across Graham's face. Viola was calling her husband's name impatiently, over and over; her voice ascending to a crescendo and then becoming low, low, much like a long, extended moan.

"Graham, Graham, Graham. What happen now?"

Mrs. Brewster turned immediately towards Viola. Then she swiveled around to face what Graham seemed to have been 'looking at'. To the right was her husband, looking helpless as he was wont to do in times like these. And to the left, standing not far behind her, leaning nonchalantly against the kitchen safe, was the long legged sixteen year old Margaret Vivian. On her face was the most malicious grin. There was no concern, no trace of apprehension, no pain. To Mrs. Brewster enquiring gaze. Margaret remarked in a cool, composed tone:

"Pa Pa seemed to have died".

It was this reaction to her father's death that persuaded Fiona Brewster that maybe Viola's feelings about her own child, Margaret Vivian was correct: She was either a lunatic or the devil incarnate.

THREE
Viola

There is no greater wealth than Virtue,
and no greater loss than to forget it.

Tiruvalluvar (c. 5th century A.D.),

THREE

Margaret Vivian and Viola were always at loggerheads. One could describe this mother and daughter relationship as 'unlikely'. Viola believed that Margaret Vivian was an angry, selfish, uncaring raging volcano of destructive energy and Margaret Vivian thought that her mother was a virago who had totally emasculated her father with her long, seething silences and her emotional demands.

For Margaret Vivian, Viola did not embody shelter, love and care as Mrs. Brewster for example. Instead, she represented for Margaret Vivian, the image of a devouring female who annihilated a person's being. She believed that her father was destroyed by this emotionally voracious woman, his wife, and therefore for him according to Margaret Vivian's reasoning, his death was a victory – an escape from the turbulence of Viola's passions.

Margaret Vivian made these severe judgments about her mother. And in truth, because of their disturbing power and their influence on her self, she inhabited a spiritually alien world, where her mother was both nurturer *and* destroyer. This ambivalence towards her mother was for Margaret Vivian, never static. It moved back and forth, back and forth, back and forth from almost intense devotion to an all encompassing hatred. She could not control these extremes of emotion, and this lack of control only exacerbated the conflict within her.

On the other hand, Viola's attitude towards Margaret was even more complex and it was so because it wasn't as easily describable......

Viola was the only girl- child of Henry and Vivian Holder. She came to them late in life and after the birth of three strong, healthy and hearty boys, she was cherished. She was spoilt – as much as poor people in a small fishing village can spoil a child. Her pampering was more of an emotional nature than a physical or material one. There were not many material possessions in her family, but there was a lot of love among members; love of one another, love of food, love of nature and a passion for the outdoors. Viola learned to share in all the wonderful and sometimes strenuous activities that marked their lives; excursions into the forest, hunting with her father and brothers, and their friend Graham, and helping her mother with the preparation of lappe and manicou that were brought to the family modest dinner table with the pride and pleasure that only country people who loved to hunt and play and eat could muster.

In other words, Viola's childhood was wonderful. Her father loved her unconditionally. Her mother spoiled her wholeheartedly and her brothers protected her with a passion that would have been difficult to surpass. So Viola grew into a young woman who was unafraid of anything and anybody. She was as happy as a lark and as free as the young blue bird she received as a gift on her sixteenth birthday. This bird was not kept in a cage as other men in the village did with their pet birds, but, CoCo, as it was called, spent most of her waking hours perched on Viola's shoulders. As the only other young female in her family, CoCo's life was blessed. She was talked to and cooed to by Viola. She flew off into the branches, but always hurried back to her perch on Viola's shoulders. So when one morning, one year after receiving her prize gift, CoCo could not be found, Viola was frantic.

It was very early on a cool August morning. Viola arose at four o'clock in order to catch the waking of the farm animals, whose loud waking noises CoCo enjoyed, since she 'sang' along with them. However, this morning, CoCo was not sitting on the arm of Viola's rocking chair.

"CoCo! CoCo!
Viola called for her little blue bird over and over again. She looked everywhere that CoCo sometimes hid. When it was rainy and cold, she slept in the cane basket, which held Viola's underclothes and which Vivian had placed in one corner of the room, under the shelf of books and magazines that her husband and Viola's brothers always brought back for her on their trips into town. Viola looked inside of her clothes shelf, where were hung her good, church clothes on pink and blue and green cloth hangers that her mother had made. CoCo was not there. Sometimes, she made a mess and hid there from Viola and from the half-hearted reprimands that Viola uttered. Becoming quite agitated, Viola ventured out into the yard to see whether CoCo had gotten outside somehow and had joined the farm animals earlier than usual, in their morning chorus. Frantic now at the disappearance of her little bird, and unwilling to wake her parents and her brothers, she ventured further afield in search of her pet.

Viola was unafraid of the dark and less nervous about being alone. As she hurried along the path into the cocoa field nearby, she called incessantly for her favourite pet. Sparky, the family's pet dog, hurried along at her side, barking occasionally at the anxiety he perceived in her voice and jumping around her in an excited way that was an indication that he sensed the concern and tearfulness of his owner.

Viola had traversed these fields many times before with her mother and father and her three brothers. Sometimes on her own, she searched for worms and bits of seeds that CoCo loved. Always, she loved to feel the moist earth beneath her bare feet and the dead leaves and fallen fruit from the trees gave that earth a heady smell that she particularly enjoyed: the earth smelt like musk and rain, and felt like soft mushy things. Sometimes the branches of the trees were wet from rain and she had to be restrained from climbing them. She particularly loved to climb a huge chenette tree that was quite close to the riverbank where the family spent much of their time during the August vacations. While her father and her older brothers worked the cocoa field, she and her mother sat on the river bank -

sometimes they washed the white clothes that needed lots of running water and the river provided this, and sometimes they just sat on the bank, and if chenette was in season, Viola ate enough to make her stomach turn. Always, she played in the cool, clean running water. The water, rippling over her feet, felt good and the small bubbles in the fast flowing pool mesmerized her. The colours of the bubbles in the water reminded her of a soapy concoction that her brothers usually prepared for her and which, when she blew out of a bamboo straw, the bubbles made big iridescent bubbles, of all colours of the rainbow; blue and red and yellow and violet and green. On these excursions, her mother never really talked much, but words were not necessary between them. They had a love and an understanding that could not be expressed in words anyway: their language was one of energy and of emotion.

It was upon the bank of this river that Viola found herself, for in her anxiety over CoCo she had traveled further afield than she had expected. Sparky was now barking incessantly, as if to warn her to turn back and go home where she would be safe. At first, she paid no attention to him. Then, he stopped the incessant noise and began to wag his tail ferociously. Viola knew she wasn't allowed this far out on her own and Sparky's barking had made her aware of how far away from home she had come. She turned back. She had not forgotten CoCo but something told her to turn back.

As she turned to go home, in the corner of her eye she saw a shadow in the distance. But she wasn't really terrified. Sparky was wagging his tail and she surmised whoever it was had to be someone she knew. There were always hunters out late – coming from the river after cleaning their catch, or some of the old men of the village, friends of her father, returning from visiting their mountain dew still, even further up the river. However, despite trying to comfort herself with these thoughts, she felt strange. She had never felt this way before in the cocoa field. She began to run in the direction of home and Sparky took off after her, now barking in excitable tones that alerted her to some danger. His ears were thrown back and he was now emitting low, loud growls that frightened her even more. Although there was a bluish light coming through the trees, which indicated the sun was about to come up over the mountains, it was still quite dark and she could not see clearly. Then she tripped on an old mango tree root and fell forward, hitting her head. As she scrambled up, she felt dazed. Her head hurt really badly and she could sense the sudden swelling between her eyes. She raised her hand to feel her face and then someone grabbed her from behind.

Sparky's loud barking hurt her head. He jumped on someone who, it seemed kicked him viciously. Yelping and growling at the same time, Sparky rushed forward again and this time, he was thrown to the ground.

She could smell the rum on the man's breath. It was a man and he was very, very strong. It passed through her mind that this was no old man. His hold on her hurt badly. In her despair, she wriggled ferociously in an attempt to free herself. Suddenly, her shoulders and her head were wrenched forward and her entire body was raised off the ground. She kicked viciously in all directions. Her terror was so great, the pain in her head so intense that she fainted.

Viola regained consciousness. Her back hurt - so did her shoulders. She felt her head and the bump was not as large as she had thought. She attempted to sit up but fell back. She lay still for a few moments and her gaze traveled upwards through the trees. The sun was not up fully, but she could see the dew on the leaves sparkling in the rays of the rising sun. The tree under which she was sprawled, looked like an overhanging bat, giving shade, but there was something ominous about it. She turned her head to the right and saw Sparky lying there whimpering. She called to him. He tried to get up, but something was wrong with one of his front legs. He just whimpered. Again, Viola tried to move towards the dog and this time, with some difficulty, she succeeded in sitting up. Her clothes were in disarray. She pulled her skirt down and attempted to stand. But as she did so, she felt dizzy. Looking down at herself, she saw blood running down her legs. She knew something was very, very, very wrong. Then she remembered the shadow and the terrifying feeling of someone holding her down. She recalled the sensations of violation and disgust - and she knew she had been raped.

Viola was mesmerized by the blood on her legs. Slowly it traveled down her legs, onto her feet and then spread out between her big toe and her other toes. She stared at her feet and the blood between her toes for a few seconds then, her body drooped down again under the tree. Her mind was in turmoil. CoCo was lost. Sparky appeared to be almost dead and her life was over before it had really begun. Strangely enough, she did not cry. Instead the first thought that came to her was, what was she going to tell her parents? Soon, if they found her missing from home, they would come looking for her. She knew they would be upset and their anxiety about her will increase their annoyance. She thought to herself;

They must not know. I can't let them find out. My brothers and father will kill every suspecting male in the village. And then what will happen; they will all go to jail and what good would that be?

Slowly she lifted her hurting body off the forest floor, and walked over to the family's pet that was lying nearby. He whimpered again as she approached and in kneeling and comforting him in his pain, her mind was able to clear itself. She touched Sparky's leg softly and realized that his bruises were not all that bad. Comforted that he was alive and will soon heal, she raised herself up again and staggered painfully the short distance to the nearby river.

The water was cold. Very cold. At this time of year, the river wasn't very deep and the water flowed easily downstream. As Viola waded until waist deep into the river, she shivered involuntarily. Her short skirt and thin blouse clung to her body. She felt dirty, unclean, and to relieve these feelings of being soiled, she waded to the middle of the river. The water quietly parted and then circled around her body. It surrounded her, engulfed her; swallowed her up.

At this time, so early in the morning, there was hardly a murmur in the forest – even the water was silent. All she could hear was the early awakening sounds of the birds in the trees above and the answering call of others as they flitted through the trees, either searching for food or bringing food to their young ones. But these were normal sounds, natural noises, and they did not disturb Viola. Slowly, she lowered her aching body into the cold water until only her neck and head were visible. She was kneeling in the water. She stretched her arms out behind her and moved them backward and forward, backward and forward, backward and forward. The water quietly whooshed against her arms and then, she began to cry.

The sound of her own sobs startled her into awareness. She seemed to come back to herself. And then she remembered again, her violation. Looking down at her legs in the clear water, she realized that the red that had oozed slowly down her legs, was moving up towards her and then away. Her life force was being slowly and steadily washed away. She watched as her blood flowed out of her and was carried downstream, mixing with the cold, cold water. She felt a great sense of loss. A feeling of deprivation and then of abhorrence shook her to the depths of her soul and then, she began to shake. This was not mere shivering from cold: It was a crumbling of her core, a spiritual collapse that affected her mind. She was in a state in which she believed that all the innocence and trust and happiness that, until now, had represented her life were obliterated – all had vanquished and were now being dissolved in her stream of tears. Viola thought of death. But what would her parents do? She was their mainstay, their life. She could and would not choose a "muddy death".

Calmly and deliberately, Viola returned to the bank of the river. She walked back to the family's pet and sat down next to him. Sparky thumped his tail in recognition of Viola's hand moving back and forth, back and forth, back and forth on his dew-drenched fur. As she sat next to the whimpering animal, Viola thought that she should return home quickly, if she was to arrive before her parents awoke. How was she to do that? Most likely, they would be awake by now, but her mother will be feeding the chickens and her father, he and her brothers, will be preparing to leave home to go to the cocoa field. Usually, she was not awake until long after they had left. She was allowed to sleep late. However, her father always peeked in at her just before he left - a habit that usually annoyed her. This morning however, she would have welcomed the intrusion. But no more. She felt desecrated and alone.

As quickly as she could, she lifted the injured dog in her arms and walked slowly and quietly towards her home. He was heavy. She was trembling from cold and to add to her discomfort, the pain that had begun in her back and head now seemed to collide and then explode in her stomach and Sparky was getting heavier by the minute.

As she came into the clearing where their house was situated, she quickly let Sparky down. He lay down for awhile. But she knew she had to move quickly now. Since the dog was so close to home, he would soon get up and limp closer to the henhouse to let her mother know that something was wrong with him. In this way, Sparky would alert Vivian that some kind of danger lurked nearby. Being the person that she was, Vivian will rush off to her husband, attempting to catch him before he left with their sons for work. Therefore, in spite of her pain Viola ran. She kept her head low and forced her legs to move as swiftly as they could to the back of the house. Her room was on the eastern side and she knew that if she crossed the yard, by passing behind the orange orchard, she should get to her room without being seen. She would scramble through her open bedroom window and lie quickly in her bed, pretending to be asleep. She knew her father would only peek and smile at her from the door and if she was lucky, he had not looked in as yet.

As she gained the safe place under the window, she could hear her mother shrieking to her husband:

"Henry, Henry! Something wrong with Sparky!!"

This was the signal for her to scramble through the window as her father and brothers would run to her mother. That divergence would give her time to pull her painful body up through the window. As she jumped up to the sill, the pain in her back threw her head backward and she almost fell to the ground. Desperately keeping her grasp on the window sill, by holding on with one hand to the curtain, she managed to heave her body forward. She hoped the curtain would not tear. She felt as though her flesh was separating from her bone, so she allowed her body to rest for a moment and then she heaved again. With a loud thud, she landed on her bedroom floor. Her back collided with the rocking chair which was placed under the window. The chair rocked back and then forward and then collapsed on its arms. Ignoring the piercing pain that passed through her body, she righted the chair with one hand and began to strip her body of the wet clothing with the other. Then, she ran to her cupboard, dragged some underclothing from the shelf and quickly changed into clean night clothes. It was after all this physical activity and the comprehension that she was safe in her room that she collapsed in tears on her soft bed.

After a short while and feeling safe now, Viola listened to the activity in the yard. She was too far away from her parents and brothers to hear their conversation distinctly but she could discern their concern for the pet dog. Then she heard the thump thump of her father's boots as he quickly rushed into her room. When he saw her lying there and seemingly so peaceful in her bed, he stopped abruptly at her door. On his approach, Viola had quickly closed her eyes, feigning sleep. Looking at him through her half closed eyes, she heard her father let out a long sigh of relief and quietly close the door.

FOUR

Vivian

Come little babe, come silly soul,
Thy father's shame, thy mother's grief.

Nicholas Breton (1542-1626),

FOUR

The baby was crying. Viola, awakened by the noise, lay unperturbed in her bed. She told herself she was too tired to pay much attention, so she turned over and fell back into a restless sleep. The baby was now three months old and did not sleep all day as before, so that now, the demanding cries of the child was for Viola, an annoyance and an aggravation.

As a result of Viola's disinterest in the child, she had never breast fed the baby. Vivian was forced to be nurturer and caregiver – not that she minded really. Hearing the screams of a hungry child coming from Viola's room, where the baby slept in a small cot, Vivian immediately dropped the needle and thread with which she was adding some delicate embroidery to the small white garment the child was to wear for her christening and hurried into Viola's room. The young baby girl was to be christened on Sunday and Vivian had a lot to do to prepare for the ritual at the small Roman Catholic Church which was situated on the beach and close to the area where the fishermen sold their catch. Vivian had to finish the small white dress. In addition, there was still preparation of the home so that she could welcome the small gathering of neighbours, who would visit after the church service. She told herself that it was fortunate that the neighbours had rallied around the family in their time of 'distress' and therefore she would not have to prepare food for the celebration meal. Her good neighbours would do that. Vivian sighed as she held the beautiful baby on her lap. The child sucked hungrily at the nipple of the feeding bottle and as she did so, Vivian's tired hand, wrinkled and lined from her hard labour, tenderly moved through the child's soft, curly hair, back and forth, back and forth, back and forth. As always, she was surprised at the unusual features of the baby; the upturned, small nose, the high cheekbones and large lips were not features that she could easily associate with Henry's family – or her own for that matter. It was always the question of origins: Who was this child's father? As she placed the baby back into her small bed, she thought that Viola had not even stirred at the insistent crying of her daughter. She had shown no interest in the baby. She was not even interested in naming the child. Vivian was tired. She had decided on her own, to call the baby Margaret, after her mother and Vivian, after herself. 'Margaret Vivian'. To Vivian, the name sounded nice.

Vivian had grown old in the passing of the last year. Her knees hurt and the doctor had attributed the breathlessness she experienced to her stress and anxiety over her silent daughter. In her few quiet moments, while she held the baby against her breast, rocking her back and forth, back and forth, back and forth on her old rocking chair, she wondered where was the opportunity for her young daughter to have gotten herself pregnant? What had she Vivian, done wrong? Notwithstanding all this guilt and hurt and pain, Vivian loved this, her first grandchild and would like to have known who her father was. Family and kin were important to her. Somehow, the baby's presence in the house had assuaged some of her pain at the loss of her husband and had lessened the loss she felt at the disappearance of the incessant chatter of her once lively daughter.

In spite of coming to terms with this unfortunate circumstance, Vivian, who was brought up in the ways of the Roman Catholic Church, was horrified that her daughter should have a child out of wedlock. It was to her an aberration – an embarrassment to the family. But an abortion would have been worse – *that* was a mortal sin. In addition, Vivian thought to herself, that at seventeen, Viola had spent no time on living; on learning to cook, to sew well and wash, to attend a few social gatherings in the village where relationships and courtships can begin and end in the ultimate achievement for any well brought up village girl – a good marriage.

Therefore, for Vivian the year was an extremely difficult one. In addition to Viola's 'shame', her husband Henry had succumbed to an illness that the doctors could not diagnose. He had whittled away gradually, becoming as thin as the rake Vivian used to sweep the leaves in the yard. Both doctors and villagers surmised that Henry's premature passing was caused by the grief that ate away at his body as well as his mind. Henry also suffered at the 'shame' of his daughter and by the time death came, Vivian was relieved that God had been merciful enough to free her hardworking husband from the pain of existence.

Viola also suffered enormously under the burden of her secret. It was on so many occasions that she had wanted to tell her family about her grave misfortune in the cocoa field a little more than a year ago. But she could not. The idea of it was too large and too traumatic for her to utter a single word. She could not bring her mind to hold on to the idea of such desecration. She had always been taught – by her father - that words concretised ideas, so that if she said anything, it would make the experience 'true'; it would become 'real'. Therefore, her repression of the occurrence was complete. As a result of the trauma she had experienced, Viola safeguarded her sanity by refusing to utter a single word more than was necessary.

That was not to say that Viola did not talk a whole lot to herself. During her pregnancy, she had cursed the child that grew larger day by day in her body. She thought of 'it' as some kind of malignant growth, a cancer that was taking over her body and which had taken control of her life. This child, which her mother refused to allow her to be rid of, was a parasite, one that fed on her body as well as a 'thing' that had eaten up her innocence. In Viola's mind her burgeoning stomach represented an enforced loss of this innocence. This abhorrent 'thing' which had deprived her of any enjoyment in her young life, was a bother, a burden, a parasite, a shame, a sin. Viola believed that her body had betrayed her by holding and keeping and sustaining an alien presence. She was pregnant – that was 'true', but that aberration would never be admitted to – by her. However, her early morning sickness; her vomiting and constant fainting substantiated to the fact of the baby's existence.

It was Viola's silence and contradictions in her behaviour that confused her family more than anything else. They did not understand her. They could not comprehend her silence. They could not cope – especially Henry. It was Henry, Viola's father who suffered the most from this tragedy. He was unable to grapple with the situation. He asked himself, 'What had happened?' 'Who was this man who had done this to his child and about whom she refused to speak?' His pain was so great that Henry, after the initial break into violence and wild rage, became morose. He too became quiet; he too spoke little to his wife, to his sons and never at all to his daughter. He could not comprehend how his beloved girl-child, she, who was so wild and talkative and energetic, had become so sullen and silent. He did not understand it. He could not understand it. He was bewildered. He was ashamed of her. He wanted to help her. But most of all, he loved her more than any other person or thing. So that when Viola dismissed his outstretched hand and his soothing words, similar to those she had used to CoCo, and given by him for comfort and in love, his world ended. He, the strong man, the good provider, the protector of his family, had succumbed to self pity and heartbreak.

At the death of their father, the three sons had lost that enormous amount of work energy which the people of the village had associated with and admired in the Holder family. Two of the boys, as young men are wont to do when they are left idle and to their own devices, drifted away from the unit of family. The older son, Mark, tried with all his strength to sustain his tired mother and his pregnant sister. However, he was not very bright and he had thought that there were many years into the future, before he would have had the responsibility of inheriting his father's farm and continuing the tradition of Fisherman and Farmer. He was not ready. His father had died too soon. Unfortunately, after Viola's misfortune and the tragic death of Henry, money was in short supply, mainly because Mark, without the support

31

of his younger brothers, could not sustain the impetus that his father was so good at doing: working hard. Although the family did not starve, the standard of living they had enjoyed in Henry's lifetime had changed dramatically.

The younger brothers, Thomas and Daniel, drifted away from the family. Thomas, the middle son, being something of an adventurer, had gone to the capital city of Port-of-Spain, where he had gotten a job as a labourer on one of the new hotels being constructed. His best friend in the village, quiet, unassuming Graham, to the surprise of everyone – even to himself - decided on the spur of the moment to accompany Thomas. However, the construction work was too hard for Graham and he returned, very soon, to the village and to his mother's small farm where he helped her rear chickens and an occasional pig for selling around Easter or Christmastime. The youngest son Daniel, who thought of himself as something of a politician, joined the Village Council group and eventually was offered the position of postman for the area. The villagers were happy to receive their mail on time, since sometimes they had to wait for weeks for the lazy postman from the nearest town to deliver the mail. In addition, Daniel could read and write quite well and since he knew everyone in the village, the letters were received by their rightful owners.

After the christening of Margaret Vivian, it seemed that Viola began to come out of herself a little. The coming together of the villagers at Vivian's house to celebrate the birth of new life in the Holder family seemed to have injected in the silent Viola, some desire to begin to communicate again. In addition, it was now becoming extremely difficult to ignore the charms of Margaret Vivian for any length of time. She screamed for attention when she was left in her bed for a long time. She demanded to be cleaned and bathed and played with. Margaret Vivian was a very demanding baby, but she was also a beautiful child. Many of the villagers remarked to her grandmother that they thought she would never be pretty – in the traditional sense

– but she would hold the attention of anyone. In other words, Margaret Vivian had, even as a baby, an arresting face and a personality to match. So as the months went by, Viola, compelled by the irresistible attraction of her daughter, began to care for her child.

In looking after Margaret Vivian, Viola got help from an unlikely source. Graham, her brother Thomas' friend was recruited by Vivian to help her older son, Mark, with the farm. The work was not extraordinarily difficult. It was the same as he did on his mother's small farm. Graham was willing to help, since he had always had a close relationship with the entire Holder family. He had no father, was an only child and therefore the three Holder boys and their father were always kind to him and good company for him. Now, Graham was good with animals and he was making a success of his mother's poultry farm. Since his poultry farm was small and did not need his attention for the entire day, he was able to assist Mark in the afternoons.

After his afternoon work sessions, Graham would remain on the Holder's farm until late evening. He usually shared their modest meals and he was good company for Mark, who never ventured far away from his mother, his sister and the new baby. It was also, to the surprise of Vivian, that Viola was quite willing to share in the evening meal when Graham was present, but they had played together as children – along with her brothers - and those happy memories may have encouraged her willingness to be sociable.

After a few months of these prolonged visits, it was soon discovered that Graham was not only good with animals, but babies seemed to like him. There was perceived to be a softness; a kind of gentleness that emanated from Graham in the presence of Margaret Vivian. The young child clung to him even more so than to her mother.

As Margaret Vivian got older and Graham stayed on the Holder's farm later, he would play rough and tumble games with the child and Viola could hear her shrieks of excitement as Graham swung her this way and that. Vivian too was happy. Graham was good company for Viola who seemed slowly to be returning to herself. And as Vivian was getting older, she could not help thinking that *maybe* Graham would make Viola a good husband: he seemed honest and kind and loving – very much as her own husband used to be. So, it was with some surprise by the villagers, but it was no surprise to Vivian that the betrothal of Viola and Graham was announced. Margaret Vivian was then almost four years old.

FIVE

Viola and Graham

… her young years bungle past
their same marriage bed
and she wishes him cripple, or poet,
or even lonely, or sometimes,
better, my lover, dead.

Anne Sexton (1928-1974) "The Farmer's Wife.")

FIVE

Josephine was born on a bright, clear Easter Sunday morning one and a half years after Graham and Viola's marriage. Everyone who visited the baby thought that she was the embodiment of the idea of an Easter baby: a peaceful child, who brought joy to all who laid eyes on her. Vivian, Viola's mother, who spent most of her time now with her newly married son, Thomas in town, thought that Josephine was quite unlike Margaret Vivian as a baby: Josephine was a pretty child with big, black sorrowful eyes that reflected an inner depth and a calm spirit. She was a quiet baby; never did she awaken her parents at ungodly hours, neither did she scream and bawl if left unattended for long periods of time. This new baby seemed to be comfortable within her self and seemed to relish being left alone. She made no fuss, even when her diapers needed changing. Therefore, her parents, her grandmother, and all the neighbours who visited often thought she was a 'good' child. This statement was always made with the knowledge of Margaret Vivian in the back of people's minds – because Margaret Vivian was thought to be the opposite.

Graham, Viola's husband and Josephine's father, relished the time spent with this undemanding child. Instead of having to comfort her at every turn, Josephine would lay quietly in the arms of her father, staring up at him with her big, beautiful black eyes. Graham rocked her back and forth, back and forth, back and forth, while he thought about the myriad chores of the next day and how to cope with them. In addition, as he rocked his young daughter on the wooden front porch and rested from the hard labour of farming, Graham would enjoy the cool, refreshing breeze of the evenings as it mixed with the wonderful smells of cooking coming from his wife Viola's kitchen. Life had been improving for the family for the last couple of years. Mark, Viola's oldest brother, had eagerly welcomed the help and continuous support on the farm that Graham's presence brought. With the death of Graham's mother, one and a half years into his marriage to Viola, Graham had sold the small farm that he had inherited and used the money to buy new, modern equipment to help him and Mark cope with the really laborious, tedious work on the Henry's property. Although, there was still a lot of back breaking work to be done, the assistance had freed Viola to be more housewife than farmer. This was ironic in itself, because Viola never liked what her husband called 'woman's work', neither was she prepared by her own parents for the long hours of drudgery in the house and in the kitchen. However, everyone was very surprised at how good she was at it. And she was. Viola was good at anything which she saw as her responsibility, but she still did not like it. As a child, she had always been a free spirit. It was her misfortune in the forest almost six years ago that had curbed her willful ways.

At her marriage to Graham, Viola seemed to have almost recovered from her trauma. She thought to herself that the sensitive, gentle Graham had a lot to do with this recovery. For Viola, Graham was able to do the impossible; he was able to make her forget the circumstances under which Margaret Vivian was conceived. Together she and Graham made, in the early days of their marriage, a wonderful home for the unusual and energetic child, for Margaret Vivian was not like other children whom they knew in the village. She walked very early and she talked continuously; the child's continuous chatter was amazing and amusing to Viola.

When Viola was at home alone with the child, she stared at her in disbelief. Margaret Vivian seemed to be a miracle, sent to her to assuage the loss of her father therefore, she transferred all the love she felt for her father onto the child. She loved her more than life itself – but she never let it show in the company of others because in truth, she did not herself understand the all-consuming emotion she felt.

She found it quite incomprehensible that Margaret Vivian, conceived under such devastating circumstances, could bring such wonderful joy to her. However, she kept her joy in this child to herself because she could not – and would not – share knowledge of her ordeal in the forest with anyone – not even Graham.

However, the difficult birth of Josephine and the early months of caring for the new baby had reminded Viola of her previous ordeal in the forest and the early months of Margaret Vivian's life. As a result, Viola had relapsed into a quiet, somnolent state. It was her good fortune that Josephine was such a 'good' baby, for there were times, during the day, when the men were away, she was able to sit and think and ponder on her present life. As she sat and rocked back and forth, back and forth, back and forth on her old rocking chair, she thought that things had not turned out too badly. What was a woman to do in circumstances like hers? She had a good husband. Some women in the village would say she had the best man in the village – and now, she had two wonderful girls – no boys – but it wasn't too late - maybe later. But Viola did not really want any more children. Viola knew that her relationship with Graham was not perfect, but he never made any great demands on her – whether physical or otherwise - and she was contented with that.

It was during one such a quiet time; a hot day in August, that Viola, as she sat thinking and rocking on the verandah, saw Graham running towards her from the orange orchard. Margaret Vivian was at school in the village and Josephine was quiet. Graham was extremely excited. Graham grabbed Viola and twirled her around and she thought something extraordinary must have happened for this behaviour was very unlike her quiet, unassuming husband. Then Viola saw her brother, Mark approaching. He too, seemed excited. Mark shouted to her:

"Vola! Viola! the man from the Agriculture Ministry has just left and he said that the cocoa field had really produced a first class yield. We should make a lot of money. Some man from overseas want all that we produce!!"

This was really good news. Mark and Graham had invested quite a sum of the farm's money from other produce into the venture to return the cocoa estate to its former productivity. If they could reap some of the rewards of their hard labour now, maybe the farm would return to the way it was during her father's life. She was glad for the two men. They had been working very hard and this turnaround would give them the break they deserved. In addition, she would be somewhat relieved to be free of the onerous task of penny pinching. Although things had been better with Graham's presence, the farm had not as yet fully recovered from her father's death.

As she rejoiced with the men, Viola was thinking that there will be money to send Margaret Vivian away to school. She was now nearly seven years old and becoming very wild, according to some of the village women who had begun to complain of her behaviour on the beach. These women thought that Margaret Vivian spent too much time with the bigger boys and seemed to be bored with girls of her own age. In truth, Margaret Vivian for the last year or so had become quite unmanageable. She had favoured Graham's mother and with her passing, she seemed to have lost her bearings. Margaret Vivian needed discipline of a 'real' school, for she had certainly outgrown the 'baby school' of the village. Viola thought it may be a good thing for her to leave the small village and go into town where she would realise that she is not, neither can she always be the centre of attention. Viola surmised that Margaret Vivian will be away from the family during the term, but she could stay with her uncle and aunt in town. They had no children and her mother Vivian, who lived with her youngest son, Thomas and his wife, will look after her. Vivian may be better able to handle the high spirited seven year old. After all, Vivian had looked after Margaret Vivian when she was a baby and she was good with children. In spite of these reassuring thoughts, Viola sighed. Viola realized that she had always loved Margaret Vivian best, but she had become wary of the child. On so many occasions lately, when she looked at Margaret Vivian, all Viola could remember was her trauma in the forest. She knew it was unfair to the child, but she could not help it. Viola thought that maybe her present feelings towards Margaret Vivian had to do with her 'wildness'. She was as wild as the forest where she was conceived.

As dusk arrived in the village, the two exuberant men, Viola's older brother Mark, and her husband Graham, had decided that they would go into town to celebrate their good news and take a few of the village men along. It was quite a rowdy group that left the village at sunset. Graham happily informed Viola that the night will be long and maybe she should not wait up as she usually did when he went into the village on Friday nights. Viola was glad to have the house to herself. She knew that Graham never drank, so she was not particularly worried about his safety. The two children were usually asleep quite early – at around nine o'clock - and she could read or sew or both according to how she felt.

The August night was very hot, so Viola left the front door open and also the door of the children's room. In this way the breeze was able to pass through the house and at the same time, she could keep an eye on the children. As she rocked steadily, back and forth, back and forth, back and forth, she stitched a new dress for Josephine, who seemed to be growing by the minute. The comforting movement of the rocking chair and the regular movement of the constrained needle, in and out, in and out, in and out of the smooth, soft fabric, reminded her of her childhood. She hoped and prayed that the quiet, meek Josephine, who loved nature, would have a happy childhood - happy as hers had been. Viola heaved a sigh and thought to herself that life was not very fair to quiet, sensitive people. Look at what had happened to her. She sighed again. Always when she was alone, she thought of the incident in the forest. It was only with Graham that she was able to forget. It was only with him that she found comfort. Soon, lulled by the comforting movement of the rocking chair, she fell asleep on the verandah. The pink garment she was sewing was draped around her knees and her hands hung loosely at her side. Suddenly, she was awakened by a loud noise. Quickly jumping to her feet, she saw a tall shadow standing in front of her. Before she even moved, she instinctively looked inside and saw Josephine curled up in her bed. Margaret Vivian was not in sight. Then there was a loud boom of a laugh and she recognized the shadow as Graham.

The sudden movement, the shadow, and the ensuing anxiety reminded her of her trauma all those years ago. Quickly she thought, would I ever forget that ... that experience? It felt like déjà vu: It took her right back to the forest when she was seventeen years old. For a moment, she did not recognize the person standing in front of her. Then she realized it was her husband. But this person was loud. His shirt was open all down to his waist. Most of it was out of his pants and the buckle of his belt was undone and made a clinking noise as he moved. He seemed to be standing on tip toe. He was swaying from side to side. Suddenly, he let out a loud belch and grinned mischievously at Viola. It was Graham, but she had never, ever seen Graham drunk before in all their years of growing up and even in their many years of marriage. Viola was horrified. She was afraid of him. Slowly, Viola moved backwards in an attempt to flee into the children's room, but Graham grabbed her from behind. And then the memories flooded back ...

She could smell the rum on the man's breath. It was a man and he was very, very strong. It passed through her mind that this was no old man. His hold on her hurt badly. Her shoulders and her head were wrenched forward and her entire body was raised off the ground. The terror was so great, the pain so intense that she fainted.....

But this time Viola did not faint. She was shocked. She recognized the hold. She relived the terror. This man was her husband and the hold was the same as that last time....

Completely disoriented and very, very frightened Viola lost her bearings. She did not run towards the children's room, as she was wont to do in times of any stress. Instead, she ran down the wooden steps and with a quiet moan lowered herself unto the dry earth near to the old wooden steps that led up to the verandah. She hid there for what seemed to be an hour, but it was really only a few minutes. As she attempted to raise herself off the dusty ground, she felt dizzy and sat down again, leaning against a wooden post that kept the steps steady. Dust had settled all over her slippered feet and on her hands and neck. She rocked her body back and forth, back and forth, back and forth. Her heart was pounding. Her arms, legs and back ached as though she had been beaten with a wooden log. She did not know why this was so and she did not really focus on it. She was too absorbed in the shock of her realization. She *knew now* that it was Graham who had raped her in the forest. *It was he.* Every instinct and the reaction of her body to his drunkenness and his touch confirmed it. Even in this state of confusion and bewilderment, she asked herself; "Why? Why would he do such a dastardly act? He wouldn't hurt a fly now, would he? Why would he, all these years ...?" She could not comprehend such betrayal. Viola felt weak, her stomach churned and she wanted to vomit. She could feel the earth moving and coming up to meet her, then moving back in a steady rhythmic movement – just like the movement of the water as she had tried to wash away the evidence; the blood of her desecration at seventeen years old.

Viola was dizzy with questions. She was stunned by Graham's treachery. She had trusted him. She had bared her soul to him. She had allowed herself to be so comfortable with him that she had revealed all her desires and hopes to him. After all, he was her husband, the father of her child. Suddenly she realized that not only was he the father of Josephine, *but he was also Margaret Vivian's father.* These ideas and thoughts were too much for her to bear at the moment. She felt sick. She had allowed herself to be taken in by Graham's pretensions. Her mind could not now grapple with the deception – not yet.

Viola could feel the sweat dripping down her face onto her neck and making its way between her breasts. Her head felt as though there was a drum inside it. The noise was so loud that she could not hear herself screaming – until she felt the child, Margaret Vivian pulling at her blouse:

"Ma Ma! Ma Ma! What happen! What happen?"

Immediately, Viola responded to the anxiety in the child's voice. She roused herself from her despair. She quieted.

She realized that she was in no state to meet or talk to her husband, so she sat on the ground beneath the steps and held Margaret Vivian close to her breast. She rocked the child, back and forth, back and forth, back and forth. Margaret Vivian was extremely frightened. She had *never* seen her mother this upset and to the seven year old, who sensed that this was not anger at her or annoyance at something that she had done, she kept very quiet and leant heavily against her mother almost as though giving her the strength that she intuited her mother needed. In addition somehow, she was happy to be there, for it was not often – or at all – that Viola held her so close.

And Viola sensing Margaret Vivian's extreme distress stroked her hair – in much the same way as she had stroked the pet dog Sparky. In doing so, her head seemed to clear. She still did not know what to do, but she knew that she had to do something. Whether she would say anything to anyone was another matter.

After a while, Viola lifted the sleeping child in her arms and slowly went up the wooden stairs. She lay Margaret Vivian down in her bed and then entered the room she shared with Graham.

Graham was sprawled across the bed. One foot was dangling off the floor and the other was bent at the knee and held under the other. He still wore the clothes that he had worn on his escapade into town. His shoes were still on.

Viola stood at the foot of the bed and looked at her husband. She stood upright. She did not lean on the bedpost or allow her body to relax. He twitched once or twice in his sleep and snored occasionally. She stood very, very still. Her arms were folded across her breast. She listened closely to his loud breathing and as she looked at him she thought about their friendship as children and their courtship.

As children they had been 'best friends'. Graham was her younger brother, Thomas' closest ally and all three of them had played and frolicked together on the beaches, in the forest and in each other's houses all their lives. Except for her brothers, Graham was the only other young male that Viola knew quite well – or at all for that matter. So when the two young men, Thomas and Graham, after the death of her father, left to go to town to work on a construction site there, she was devastated.

At the return of Graham, a few weeks later, because, as he had said, he was unable to handle the difficult task of a labourer, Viola was very happy. Although she did not speak to him at all on his return, he would sometimes sit on their verandah with her mother. She used to hear them talking softly together as Graham had attempted to comfort Vivian as she tried to deal with Viola's misfortune. She had always thought that his kindness was due to their shared childhood experiences and the love that had developed among herself, her three brothers and Graham. *She knew now that he wasn't what she thought he was. He was a traitor, a betrayer, a man without conscience.*

To relieve the ache in her heart and the pain in her legs, Viola lowered her tired body onto her old rocking chair which was placed close to the bed. For a few minutes, she closed her eyes as she rocked back and forth, back and forth, back and forth. The old chair creaked under her weight, but Vivian did not hear the noise. Then she opened her eyes and stared at the inert body of her sleeping husband as he lay sprawled on the bed in his drunken stupor. Hatred welled up in her heart. Her mouth became filled with liquid and her immediate reaction was to empty its contents onto the sleeping man; to spatter his face with the bile that rushed up from her stomach and into her mouth. Instead, she swallowed and then, she began to cry. The quiet tears she shed were not only tears of helplessness and grief, but also those that came from an inexorable anger. Graham had committed the worst act against *any* woman: He had taken advantage of her physical vulnerability. He had deprived her of her innocence. *He, whom she had loved as a brother, who had gained the respect and admiration of her parents, who had comforted her in times of distress, to whom she had revealed all her girlish secrets and later in marriage, demonstrated her womanly wiles, he had, all this time, been the source of all her distress.* She could not believe it. She was devastated. The betrayal was complete. And because the betrayal was so significant and overwhelming, the only way she knew of dealing with it, was to go back within herself; to become quiet, to withdraw, because the skills of coping with such a tragedy did not exist for her. Not knowing what to do Viola reverted to silence. She could not speak. She had to think. She had to know for sure. She had to wake up her husband. *She had to act.*

Raising herself off the rocking chair, Viola moved quickly towards the bed and stood close to the side nearest to where Graham was stretched out. She knew if she had to do this, she had to do it quickly. Bracing herself, by opening her legs wide, she placed her feet squarely on the wooden floor. Leaning over the snoring man, she raised her right hand and slapped Graham with all the strength she could muster. She slapped him three times. At the first slap, Graham merely groaned. At the second slap, he attempted to raise himself off the bed, but collapsed heavily back onto the mattress. The third slap aroused him. He turned on his side and his eyes flew open. He was in a daze and when he saw Viola towering over him, he knew. Graham mumbled something incoherently and then Viola hit him again, this time with the back of her hand. He almost fell off the bed. Graham sat up suddenly and stared at Viola in shock:

"Wha ...aaa ...t! Whaaa...t!!"

His face was marked by the creases of the pillow case and now it was flushed red by Viola's onslaught.

Speaking slowly, Viola said to Graham;

"Get off the bed and sit on the rocking chair."

Viola kicked the rocking chair closer to the bed so that Graham, with one movement could have slid off the bed and onto the chair. However, in his still drunken state, he missed the chair and he and the chair collapsed onto the floor. The chair fell on top of him. Viola righted the chair and Graham raised himself off the floor. He sat on the edge of the bed, looking up at Viola, at her angry, unrecognizable face. Graham knew that Viola had discovered his secret. He stretched out his hand to her and Viola quickly moved away from him. Graham began to cry. Loud nasal noises escaped from his mouth and these awful sounds, startled Viola. However, surprisingly, in spite of his distress, Viola realized that Graham looked relieved. He suddenly looked like a man who was freed of a great burden. Graham's shoulders were drooped and his head sagged onto his chest. His arms were lying heavily on his lap, but his voice was quite clear as he began to talk.

It was weird. Graham's voice was not much over a whisper, but strangely it carried clearly to where viola was standing, near the window to allow herself some fresh air. Graham began slowly, and then his words began to flow from his mouth quickly. They were interspersed with lengthy silences as though he was, for the first time, attempting to articulate his reckless behaviour:

"You cannot know what it has been like …. All these years… I have been living in hell. ….. All these years … to be treacherous to the people who loved you most, who cared for you, who trusted you …. And whom you love. I am lost. I know I am lost. I cannot look at myself … You don't know what it is like …..harbouring this secret … my wife, my mother, my girl children, my friends, my friend's sister …. Viola, I am sorry … I know I am a coward … You don't know what it is like".

Graham swallowed nervously and then continued,

"I always knew I could not drink … That is why, all these years I have not done so …Have you ever seem me drunk? I know what it does to me …I don't understand it …Why? … Why do I turn into a beast …? What is it? You don't know what it is like. I cannot tell you about the disgusting act I committed because I do not understand why ….. I know your father would have killed me …. I know your brothers would have crucified me … And I deserve to be. But I wanted to live

Viola ... I did not want to die ..... I was young ... And later, it was too late ... I could not tell ....

You must believe me when I say I truly love Margaret Vivian. I always knew she was my own .... She looks like my grandmother ... and I thought I could help you.... Your family to cope .... I knew this is my fault.... But I wanted to live ... I did not want to die... I wanted to live... I Do.....

Graham's voice trailed into nothingness In all her despair the thought occurred to Viola that Graham's last two words were significant; they were the same ones he had uttered so quietly, but with so much confidence, near the riverbank where they were married so many years ago. It was a beautiful ceremony. Graham had looked so tall, so handsome, so confident. And now looking at him, what she saw was a paltry figure; a mere shadow of that former, strong, confident man. He looked more like her own father at the end of his days - - battered and defeated. As she remembered her father, she realized that that it was this man who was sitting before her who was responsible for his untimely demise. Graham had killed her father.

Then she thought that the memory of what Graham had done had almost killed him as well. It had changed him in ways that if she was paying attention, she would have perceived the deterioration. All these years .... Viola remained quiet for a long, long time. She roused herself eventually and looked at the woe-begotten man slumped before her. Walking around the room cleared her mind. She walked to the dressing table, picked up her hairbrush, placed in its correct position. She covered the powder bowl and straightened the little white doily under the perfumed bottles. Surprisingly, all the anger had drained out of her body and with it flowed all the feeling she had ever had for Graham. She looked at him and did not even feel pity. There was nothing she wanted to say to him. She felt no urge to ask him ... why? Anyway, he had said he did not understand..... She thought to herself, his explanation – if that was what that was – could stand. It did not matter. Not now. At that precise moment, Viola decided that her life would comprise herself and her two children. Her marriage had ended. It was finished. Graham could go - or he could stay.

Viola had come to the conclusion that not knowing who was responsible for her misfortune may have saved her psychologically. She did not think that at the age of seventeen, she could have coped with the knowledge of Graham's transgression. She thought that too much had been left unsaid for too long. Maybe, she mused, it should remain unsaid. She shook her head from side to side and contemplated what good will this knowledge serve .... *now?*

Viola looked across at Graham. He was sitting very still in the old rocking chair. He neither raised his head to look at her nor did he glance at his image in the mirror placed above the night table. Viola turned away from the dressing table, and without glancing again at Graham, walked out of their bedroom. As she slowly walked out of the room, Viola did not see Margaret Vivian hiding behind the door.

SIX

Margaret Vivian

As for me, I am mean: that means that I need the
suffering of others to exist.
A flame. A flame in their hearts. When I am all alone, I am extinguished

Jan Paul Sartre

No Exit *[act 1 sc. 5]*

SIX

I was always an obdurate child and to be successful at that, I was aided by a wonderful gift: I possessed a phenomenal memory. As a result, the 'conversation' – if you wish to call it that – between my mother and Pa Pa - my father - was, and still is the clearest and most traumatic memory of my life. That incident was a good indicator of the distressing and the dysfunctional manner in which my parents communicated. Unfortunately, I cannot remember any other way through which our family communicated: There were always long silences, long intense periods of quiet – and no laughter. My mother's persistent taciturnity was what made these experiences so uncomfortable. Her ways of behaving in the house – and outside it - were always stressful to the rest of the family. And as time passed, it got worse. These long silences infuriated me. Her sullenness irritated me. It seemed to me – even now when I remember her behaviour on that night - and her demeanour for long years afterwards - that my mother took pleasure in the torture the rest of the family suffered. In some perverse way, my mother took power from everyone through perfecting the performance of the 'suffering wife'.

Never, to my knowledge had she uttered a word to anyone about what had happened in Pa Pa and her bedroom that fateful night. It was left unsaid. Always the self-righteous woman – the 'wronged' woman, her behaviour always provoked me into behaving in ways that even to myself was objectionable. I know that many people in our village – and even in our family thought I was an 'aberration' – because of my behaviour. And I know that it had to start somewhere. I believe my behaviour began to deteriorate on the night I heard about the manner in which I was conceived.

It was eight o'clock on that fateful night and my mother was in her usual place; rocking back and forth, back and forth, back and forth on her old rocking chair on the wooden verandah. She thought that I was asleep, but I had left the bedroom which I shared with my baby sister Josephine and had slipped into my parents' room to read. I loved to read. A light was always left on in that room, as long as my father was out. My mother usually sat on the verandah, rocking and awaiting his return. Whenever my parents were away from their bedroom on these Friday nights, I would sneak into their bed and lie on their big comfortable bed with the lamp turned towards my head [Always I lay with my head at the foot of the bed in order not to rumple the pillows, for if my mother found out, she would nag on and on forever].

Usually, I would hear my father's return because my Uncle Mark would drop him off after their Friday night outings. Then I would quickly straighten the sheets and scuttle back quickly to my own narrow bed. But on this particular Friday night, I was caught up in the book I was reading. It was about a young girl who had lost her parents in a fire and the Angels of Mercy, representing her guardian angels, had taken her up into the sky away from all her pain and sorrow. I felt like I knew this girl because the way she reacted to her misfortune, before the angels came to her rescue, was the way I felt in my mother's presence; bereft of love and deprived of compassion.

Also, because I was absorbed in my book, I missed the late night goodbyes between Uncle Mark and Pa Pa. What I did hear was a booming guffaw and then a loud noise as though someone had tripped and had fallen over coming up the stairs. I stopped reading for a minute and listened. There was silence. Then I heard an anxious cry in my mother's voice: It sounded as though she was in pain. Bewildered by such a sound coming from my always self-possessed mother, I quickly jumped off the bed and anxiously peered through the window. I saw my mother stumbling down the wooden stairs. She looked so unlike her normal composed self, that I immediately became frightened. Careless about straightening the sheets on the bed, I dashed out of the room and followed her. She was sitting crumpled over, under the wooden verandah. I stood quietly watching and then ran forward towards her, not because I felt the urge to comfort her, but because my fright overcame my inhibitions. Overhead, I could hear my father's footsteps, as he stomped noisily from the bathroom to his bedroom.

Sensing my fear and in response to my anguish, my mother, for the first time that I could remember, drew me close and held me tightly to her breast, as she rocked back and forth, back and forth, back and forth – just as she did on her rocking chair. This physical closeness to my mother was, for me, even more frightening than the unusual, strange noises Pa Pa had made and the strangling sound that had escaped from my mother's lips. She held me so tight that I felt as though I was being stifled, but I did not move. We stayed like that for a long time. Then abruptly, my mother got up and taking my hand, she walked me, very, very slowly, back to my room. Josephine, the baby, had not stirred.

As soon as she left, I darted back into my mother's room in an attempt to straighten the bed clothes before she discovered that I had been on her bed. I was too late. Pa Pa was sprawled on the bed – with his shoes on – and my mother was coming into the room. To avoid her, I darted under the bed. No one knew I was there. I remained as quiet as I could. I held my breath, for I was afraid my mother would hear me breathing. She too was very quiet for a very, very long time. I began to wonder what she was doing for my legs were cramped and I wanted to sneeze from the dust. I wanted to get out from under the bed. Then, at last, I heard her speak: She asked my father to get up. I did not recognize her voice. She was speaking in this strange tone. I sneezed – softly. Then I heard loud, slapping noises. Not much later, I heard my father crying. I was shocked and overwhelmed with fear. I could not move. I was paralysed.

What I heard my father say was unbelievable. I could not understand it all, but what I heard, I could not believe. I knew it had something to do with sex. Even at eight years old, I knew all about sex. I had grown up on a farm and what my father was saying seem to have something to do with that, but it sounded awful, seeming to be something unnatural and sinister. I listened closely and did not recognize that voice as that of my Pa Pa. In addition, what he was saying was unthinkable. The knowledge was incredible enough, but the pain with which the words were uttered was too much for me to bear. It was not possible that my father could have done these things to my mother. He was not some beast, some pig or goat. He was my Pa Pa. I could not listen anymore. I knew I was intruding on some private talk, so I placed my hands over my ears, pulled my feet up to my chest and closed my eyes. Soon after, the room went very, very quiet. Carefully, I peeped out from my hiding place and saw my mother slowly leaving the room. It was then that I scrambled from under the bed and hid behind the door. Pa Pa had not moved.

The next morning, my mother was in the kitchen as usual. Quiet and contained, she looked after my little sister's meals and prepared the vegetables for lunch. She frightened me. Her entire body was tight. Not a muscle moved in her face. Not a smile, not a grin – not even a smirk. And my Pa Pa looked lost. He did not go to the cocoa estate that morning, but sat around the house – forlorn. I felt his pain. He was my Pa Pa and his hurt showed in every muscle of his body. He was pathetic to watch. I wanted to kill my mother. I knew somehow that she was responsible for this change in my father. I hated my mother. I would have killed her if that was possible. I did not understand what was happening to our family. As I grew older and recalled the incident over and over again, the more I understood. But at that time I could forgive my father anything; he loved me, he played with me and treated me with respect. He was my only consolation. My mother, on the other hand, was so distant. From my very early years, the only person I could remember who always listened to me was my father and my grandmother, Vivian. But now Gran Vivian was sick and lived in town with Uncle Thomas and his new wife.

53

I have never said anything to my mother or my father. I never let them know that I had heard their secret and I suffered long and hard for not sharing that knowledge – all through my school days – through the death of my Pa Pa, when I was fifteen.

Never would Margaret Vivian's cynical, candid eye - and ear - allow her to resolve the discords of her existence into a smooth and easy coherence. Margaret Vivian had decided early in her young life – although she might not have expressed it thus then, that *her* life was *not* going to follow the mundane path of the women around her. She would make sure that the dullness and obscurity that governed the lives of these other women in the village – especially her mother's - would not be her experience. Her life will not be capricious and confused. Her life will have form and function: there will be no frantic, busy movements that were directionless and unproductive in *her* life making it unnoticed and dull. \

Since Margaret Vivian believed she understood – fully - the conditions of living in a small fishing village, she resolved to do *whatever was necessary* to turn her time on Earth into the most interesting and exquisite account. Therefore, Margaret Vivian tried very, very hard, to make her life different.

Firstly, it must be said that Mrs. Brewster's opinion of Margaret Vivian at the death of her father had much validity. Margaret Vivian behaved towards everyone in the village as though she was a law unto herself: She completely ignored her younger sister, Josephine, who she thought was 'silly and foolish'. Josephine was quiet: subdued in her behaviour and restrained in her expressions, she was really the opposite of Margaret Vivian. Sedate and accommodating, she usually moved with the flow of emotion in the house, thereby adapting her behaviours to its requirements. However, in one particular aspect of their responses to situations, the two sisters saw eye to eye: They both had a deep and unrelenting dislike for their mother.

In Josephine's case, her dislike was easily explained; she objected bitterly to the way her mother treated her beloved father. But for Margaret Vivian, her dislike for her mother was complex; it manifested itself as a loathing – an abhorrence of the woman herself. Having more information than Josephine about her mother's history with her father, that is, knowledge about the conception of her own birth, her dislike went beyond the situation itself and was based prominently on her mother's self-indulgent attitude; the way her mother, indignant and self-righteous, reveled in her own past misfortune.

Secondly, it must also be said that those qualities which Margaret Vivian thought to be reprehensible in her younger sister; her sedateness and her obliging nature, were attributes that most members of the village believed to be qualities that made young girls into good women. Patience, respect for your elders, a form of serenity that allowed young girls to be obtrusive; that is to be seen and not heard, hardworking and most of all, compliant. These were virtues to be admired and emulated. So that the longer Margaret Vivian lived with her detached, unfeeling mother and her accommodating sister, the more rebellious she became. Thus, following the sudden death of her father, she was taxied out from her home and sent to stay in town with her grandmother and her uncle, mainly because it was thought that she needed a strong male hand to keep her in check [and her uncle was to provide this hand].

In addition, whatever was said about Margaret Vivian by other villagers and however much she disliked her sister's attitude [because she knew she could not depend on her for support – especially emotional – in any conflict with their mother] they all knew she was of superior intelligence. The only teacher in their village, Teacher Phyllis, believed that Margaret Vivian had a 'fine mind' and would benefit from further education.

All these thoughts and ideas were important in Margaret Vivian's ejection from her home, but the deciding factor that led to Margaret Vivian's expulsion from the only place she knew as home was the death of her father. At Graham's death, Viola could no longer stand the sight of her first child. She told herself that if Margaret Vivian was out of sight, then maybe ... maybe ... she would be able to wipe the experience of that traumatic incident that happened at seventeen from her mind ... just as she had almost succeeded in forgetting about her pregnancy – until her body harbouring a mystifying presence, produced the 'aberration' that was Margaret Vivian. Thus, unable to understand her reactions to Margaret Vivian, Viola tried to reason with herself. Margaret Vivian was present there, all these years *after* she had discovered who her father was. Why was it *now*, at Graham's death that the child appeared to be an even greater abomination in her sight? Viola could not comprehend the reasons why. She could not unravel this mystery. The fact was that Viola could not, in any true sense, separate the hate she felt for Graham with the inexpressible love she held for her first child. For Viola, there was no way of reconciling such hate and such all consuming love and as a consequence, to save her sanity, she withdrew even further from Margaret Vivian, back into her cold, silent world.

And Margaret Vivian knew full well - for she was not stupid. She felt she knew *why* Viola was so eager to be rid of her: Viola wanted to be rid of anything or anyone that reminded her of Graham and *that* incident. She had gotten rid of Graham – in his death – and therefore, if Margaret Vivian was no longer present – not dead [God Forbid!] but away somewhere, anywhere, she would not have to deal daily with the outcome of her trauma.

Viola knew that the ambivalence she experienced towards her first child was unreasonable and irrational. It would seem so to anybody– with any sense. But she could not help it: It seemed insane. But unable to come to terms with the contradictions of her own feelings towards Margaret Vivian; the sudden feelings of hate, the almost all-consuming love she felt sometimes, she made up her mind that if the girl was away from her, she may be able to control the constant and emotionally debilitating stress and conflict; love, hate, love, hate, love hate – back and forth, back and forth, back and forth.

Margaret Vivian's stay in the town Sangre Brito was an unusual and an eventful one. She spent six months at her uncle's home, before she was sent to school. She was bored. Her grandmother, was still as talkative as ever, but she wasn't very well and therefore spent most of her time in bed or sitting on the verandah rocking herself in her old rocking chair, or visiting her old doctor friend who fed her herbs of all kinds in order to relieve her many ailments. In addition, Margaret Vivian did not get along with her uncle's young wife, whose family lived three houses down the street and with whom she preferred to spend all of her free time. Therefore, Margaret Vivian got even less supervision than she did in her home village. As a consequence of these circumstances, her Uncle Thomas, having to travel far to his job and returning late at night, decided to place her in the convent school where the education was thought to be superior and where she could remain until six o'clock on evenings. Thomas thought that if the nuns lived up to their reputation, when Margaret returned home from school, she would be too tired to do anything else but sleep. So, at fifteen and a half years old, having sat the school's entrance examination, Margaret was placed in a Form three class.

Big for her age and unruly to boot, Margaret Vivian proved to be the undoing of many young students in her class. Many of the young girls – mostly Roman Catholic and carefully chosen for a prestigious place in the convent school – talked among themselves. They thought that Margaret Vivian was unsuitable for such a place, but they knew that her uncle was a good member of the church who donated financially to many of the various charities that the nuns were interested in.

Only two months into attending the convent school and Margaret Vivian disliked many of the nuns. She believed that most of them were as hypocritical and as pretentious as her mother. She thought that the posturing among these women made it difficult for anyone to be really fond of any of them – except Sister Sarah Rose who seemed sympathetic to the plight of some girls who were experiencing difficulty at home. Sister Sarah Rose exhibited an earnestness and conviction to purpose that exuded from her small frame. She was an intensely religious, very sincere woman and seemed to have the uncanny ability to read Margaret Vivian's mind. Sister Sarah Rose taught the girls both English and French. Since Margaret Vivian was a voracious reader and a lover of literature, she was always attentive in her classes, as opposed to the ruckus she created and the objectionable behaviour she exhibited in many other classes.

It was not known to Margaret Vivian – although she may have suspected it - that Sister Sarah Rose saw in her, a kindred spirit. Actually, both these female figures, recognized in each other an ability to think deeply and imagine fiercely, but they dealt differently with their angst. In terms of conduct, Margaret Vivian had developed ways of coping with the trials and tribulations in her life that seemed to bring out the worse in her: She was rude and wild. Sister Sarah Rose, on the other hand, had learned early in her life to repress and subdue her wild impulses. She had joined the convent because she recognized that in religion, she could sublimate her wild ideas and thoughts through an obedience to God and through service. As a result of this likeness, Sister Sarah Rose was the only person whom Margaret grew to love and respect.

In addition, Margaret Vivian had made two close friends in her class; Clarissa Martin and Yvonne Clarendon. The girls were close to her own age: Clarissa was fourteen years old and her parents were overseas 'in the States'. Clarissa lived in a very unrestricted family arrangement, in which her grandfather, not very old - and young enough to believe that he still had a lot to live for - was the adult. Also, Clarissa's two young aunts, both under the age of twenty five, were more concerned with getting ahead in life; in the sense that they were more interested in making themselves ready for the marriage market, than in supervising their young niece. The other girl Yvonne, was Margaret Vivian's choice for what she termed 'her best friend'. She was the same age as Margaret Vivian – short of two months. A very assertive young woman, Yvonne was the oldest child in her family and was accustomed to being the boss to her six brothers and sisters. She too, was very bright at school. Always first in class, she perceived a real competitor in Margaret Vivian and in order to keep her first place, she deliberately decided to befriend her. At first, these two young girls fought - only once physically – to remain the premium student, until realizing that they were equally matched, they decided to join forces. Yvonne, in one of her quieter moments, as she planned strategy to 'overthrow Margaret Vivian,' as brightest and best in class, came to the conclusion that it "is better to join them that to fight them'. These two girls became very good friends and their friendship lasted into early adulthood.

It was on the last day of their school years that Margaret Vivian, at eighteen years old, decided to culminate her school experience by doing something which would be remembered by both nuns and students for many years to come. Both Clarissa and Yvonne were part of the initial planning. However, these two girls were only privy to part of the plan. Margaret Vivian was intent on revealing the entire plan to her friends at the last minute. She told herself she had to 'score'. She would show those nuns what she was made of .....

It was three o'clock on the last day of school. All examinations were over and the girls were having a good time; talking and laughing and exaggerating what they would be doing before they went off to work or to further study. Margaret Vivian, Clarissa and Yvonne were participating in these inventions, but soon Margaret Vivian in particular, became bored of the fantasies. She decided that she was ready to put her plan into action. Leaving the group of daydreaming girls and dodging her two friends, Margaret Vivian ran from the school and into the church. She had brought from home, a mixture of different herbs, a thick potion that her grandmother, Viola, had simmering on the stove as a remedy for her painful knees. It was a thick, red, clumpy stuff that could cling to flesh even without bandages. Usually Vivian would soak her knees with the potion and then wound bandages around them. She said that they kept her knees cool for long periods at a time. What Margaret Vivian knew is that they stained her grandmother's knees bright red. She always looked as though her knees were bleeding.

Margaret carried a small can filled with her grandmother's potion. She had placed it in her school bag and tiptoed out of the house while her grandmother was still in bed. She had thought that since school was finished, she could easily hide the stuff in her bag, because there were no books to carry or to get messed up - if the substance happened to spill. Now, swiftly speeding up the aisle of the small church, she sat on the first pew in front of the altar and carefully removed the potion from her bag. As she was intent on her task, Father Peters walked out from the sacristy and looked at her suspiciously. Immediately, she dropped to her knees and quietly waved to him, as she uttered quietly;

"Good Afternoon Father"

Father Peters looked at her curiously, but he continued on his way out of the church. He did not have much to do or say to the school girls. He thought that they were, in the main, a group of uncivilised, aggressive young women who were the responsibility of the nuns of the parish. The priest slowly walked to the front of the altar, genuflected, then he raised himself from his knees and with his arm folded, he walked out of the church. It was enough time for Margaret Vivian to rethink the sacrilege that she was about to commit. However, it was not in her nature to rethink anything, so she waited patiently for Father Stephens to disappear around the corner of the church and enter his car. She was sure that he could not distinguish her from any of the older girls and thus, she thought she was safe.

At six ten in the evening, Sister Sarah Rose, on her way to chapel to place fresh flowers at the foot of the statue of the Virgin Mary, walked up the aisle of the church. She was thinking about this last group of girls who had spent their last day at school today. She thought that they were a good group - as students go nowadays. Most of them had come from good families and they would do well she knew, when the examination results were released in a couple of months. Then her mind turned to Margaret Vivian and she sighed. She hoped that after the final blessing tomorrow, when the graduating class gathered, that she could have a final word with Margaret Vivian. She sighed again. She regretted that she did not have greater influence on the child, but the girl was wild and extremely difficult to control. She knew that Margaret Vivian behaved quite well in her classes, but the same could not be said for her behaviour in the classes of some of the other nuns – particularly Sister Anne Marie. The girl hated the nun. It was true that Anne Marie was intolerant of any behaviour that she thought was 'different', but the words she used to describe Margaret Vivian were in the extreme; uncultured, uncouth, coarse. The matter would have been funny if it wasn't so serious. Margaret Rose sighed again as she knelt before the statue of the Virgin Mary. She was about to cross herself, when she uttered a loud cry. In dismay she whispered;
"O my Lord, O my Lord. Help us!"

The bouquet of yellow and white roses fell from her hands. She half rose from her knees and then collapsed onto them again. Her face became as red as the altar cloth. She began to breathe loudly. She held one hand flat against her chest as though that action near her heart could quiet the loud noise that emanated from her chest. She thought her body was about to explode. Heat radiated from her body. Her hands were wet with perspiration and she could feel the water dripping down the centre of her back – like a rivulet in full flow.

As she attempted to stand, she stepped on her robe and almost fell forward. She righted herself and held onto a pew to catch her breath. She could not believe what she was seeing. She rubbed her eyes and then again. In front of her was the statue of the Virgin Mary. But something was very, very wrong; blood was flowing from Her eyes, from Her hands and from Her feet. It was incredulous. Then Sister Margaret Rose threw herself prostrate on the ground before the Virgin Mary and began to wail.

Sister Anne Marie and two other nuns, Sister Martha and Sister Camille Jane, who heard the loud wailing, dropped the white tulle fabric with which they were working in the nearby presbytery, making rosettes for the students' graduation the next day. They ran as fast as they could towards the noise. It seemed to be coming from the chapel. As they entered the church and quickly genuflected at the open door, they saw Sister Sarah Rose, in front of the altar, lying prostrate before the Virgin Mary. She seemed to have fainted. Quickly, they ran towards her and attempted to lift her up off the floor. Sister Sarah Rose was a small woman, but she was limp – like dead weight, a rag doll – and the nuns were having some difficulty in raising her up off the floor. With one sudden movement , they were about to place the drooping figure of Sister Margaret Rose on the nearest pew, when Sister Camille Jane, the oldest of the three nuns, gave a loud cry and let go off her load. Sister Sarah Rose fell back onto the floor. Annoyed at her sister nun's careless hold, her voice irritable, Sister Anne Marie was about to shout at her, when she looked to where the other nun was pointing; her hands were outstretched, her fingers curled back except for her forefinger. Sr. Camille Jane was pointing towards the figurine of the Virgin. Her body trembled and her finger wagged as though she was chastising a young student. Sister Anne Marie looked up and saw blood flowing from the eyes of the figure. It streamed down the breast of the statue. It covered the tightly clasped hands of the image and dripped very slowly, in a heavy slow stream, down the front of its white robe and onto the bare feet of the Virgin Mary. Like globs of a heavy tar-like potion, it descended in a pool and settled at the foot of the raised statue. Sister Anne Marie stood erect. She could not move. Her mouth remained open. She looked like a woman about to scream but no sound came out of her mouth. Being a woman who always moved deliberately and with precision, she carefully lowered the weight of Sister Sarah Rose that she was now bearing alone, onto the pew. Sister Sarah Rose drooped on to the pew and her lank arms fell into her lap. Her head rested on her breast like a sorrowful, mournful repentant. Then Sister Anne Marie looked across at Sr. Camille Jane who was sitting in a daze; her many garments caught between her legs. She was leaning against the long communion rail that surrounded the altar. Sister Anne Marie lowered herself to her knees in front of the statue, close to where Sister Camille Jane sat. Sister Martha had long ago escaped from the church.

After the hysterical finger pointing of Sr. Camille Jane, not a single word or cry had been uttered. The chapel was now very quiet. After a few moments, Sister Anne Marie got up off her knees and with her knees visibly shaking, she, walked out of the chapel. She seemed to have forgotten both Sister Margaret Rose, who sat as though in prayer in the pew and Sister Camille Jane, who remained lost in some kind of trance.

Early the next morning, the large crowd that had gathered outside of the convent could not be contained. The noise these people were making was in direct contrast to the former quiet movements of Sister Anne Marie as she had left the chapel the day before. Father Peters was informed of the miracle of course, and he had informed the archbishop. Who had told the press – nobody knew.

Margaret Vivian had awakened early on that last day of school. She felt very excited and wondered why. Then she remembered the caper of the day before. She laughed to herself as she hurried through her breakfast and her dressing. She had heard her grandmother calling to her as she went through the door, but she did not stop to find out what she wanted. She shouted back at her;

"I'm late for school Granny. See you later!"

Her grandmother sighed at the impetuousness of the young, turned on her side, for she wasn't feeling very well that day, and went back to sleep.

Margaret Vivian bolted through the front door. She could not wait to meet her two friends Clarissa and Yvonne and tell them about her daring act in the chapel the day before. She laughed to herself and thought that this one would top them all. She wanted to go out with a bang – to leave school with memories that would carry her for a while. She laughed again as she boarded the bus at Wilton Corner. The ride to school was a short one, but today it seemed to be taking a very long time. As the bus approached her usual stop, she saw a large crowd gathered outside the convent and wondered what had happened. Descending from the bus, she pushed herself through the noisy crowd. Some people were shouting and others were very quiet. An old lady in a wide straw hat kept repeatedly crossing herself. Margaret Vivian began to wonder what all the excitement was about. As she approached the school gates, she saw that they were locked but she could see Clarissa and Yvonne, among a large group of her classmates, standing inside the gates. Curious to find out what was happening, she ran a bit further up the road and squeezed through the small hole in the fence, which the girls used as a getaway if they did not want to be discovered leaving the school yard during school time. A she joined her friends in the convent yard, she realised that they seemed very subdued and she wondered if one of the nuns had died. She hoped it was Sister Anne Marie.

In the excitement of the moment, even Margaret Vivian had forgotten what she had done the day before. Something extremely important seemed to have happened. Then she thought to herself that this would happen to her. Now, her surprise would fade into the background. She was just about to question her friends Clarissa and Yvonne on what the commotion was all about, when, Maria Brendon, one of the really religious girls, without being asked, began in excited tones, to relate about the "miracle of the Virgin Mary" All the girls gathered around her. Some were excited, some seemed to be afraid and others looked on in pure wonderment or in dismay. Clarissa and Yvonne belonged to this last group. Clarissa was very excited. She was holding on tightly to two other girls and they continually crossed themselves. Yvonne, on the other hand, was dismayed. Because of conversations she had had with Margaret Vivian the day before, she suspected that somehow, in some way, Margaret Vivian was responsible for this spectacle. She was sure that this fiasco was *her* fault. Yvonne thought that this time Margaret Vivian had gone too far. There must be a limit to what people would do in the name of 'fun'. Margaret Vivian did not have to tell her that she was responsible for this sacrilege. One look at her face after she was told what every one was so excited about, told its own story. Margaret Vivian had burst out laughing. *She* was the culprit. It was she who had committed this blasphemy in the chapel... Yvonne knew this intuitively and was terrified of her friend. She thought to herself what manner of person would do such a reckless thing? Did she not have a conscience – no respect for what other people held dear?

As Margaret Vivian was about to expose her scam, Yvonne, gripping her arm tightly, dragged her away from the group of frightened girls. Margaret was protesting loudly, but the other girls did not pay attention to her, they had crowded around Sister Margaret Rose who was attempting to usher them quickly into the chapel. Now, it was only Margaret Vivian and Yvonne standing in the school yard and Yvonne did not appear to Margaret Vivian to be her normal self:

Now what could possibly make Yvonne so upset? It was only a joke. She knew we were going to do something extraordinary. I bet she is annoyed because she wasn't in on it from the beginning. Well too bad. She looks frightened! Is she afraid of me? It was only a joke!

Looking at Margaret Vivian again, Yvonne realized that she was out of control. For the first time Yvonne saw what many of the other girls in the class had perceived in Margaret Vivian all these years. Yvonne realized that Margaret Vivian had no limits.

SEVEN

Viola and Margaret Vivian

Nature is beneficent. I praise her and all her works. She is silent and wise. She is cunning, but for good ends. She has brought me here and will also lead me away. She may scold me, but she will not hate her work. I trust her.

Johann Wolfgang von Goethe

SEVEN

After the fiasco on the last day of school and the scandalous, detailed reports in the newspapers about the practical joke, it was believed by most of the public that the school girls at the convent school had played in the chapel, many of Margaret Vivian's peers had refused to speak with her. They *knew* that she was the one responsible and they did not care to be associated with such a dastardly act. Even Clarissa had decided that Margaret Vivian wasn't worth the loss of her reputation and she abandoned their friendship. It was only Yvonne who visited her at her uncle's home during the August vacation – although her visits were quite infrequent and eventually those visits also petered out.

As a result of her behaviour, Margaret Vivian was not welcome anywhere in the town, for rumour had spread quickly that she was the culprit and in a small town of not many people – a number of whom were Roman Catholic - Margaret Vivian was thought of as being the devil incarnate. She could not get a 'summer job' and in order to keep her out of more trouble, her uncle drove her back to her village – and deposited her at her mother Viola's front door.

On her return, Margaret Vivian sat around the house. She neither helped her mother and younger sister Josephine on the farm, nor did she do any housework. She did not cook, wash or clean house. She knew within herself that she needed to keep herself busy, but she was bored; she was bored with the women and young girls in the village, who, when they gathered, talked about their clothes, their children or their menfolk and when one or two of their group were missing, they spent much time gossiping and maligning those who were not present.

However, in spite of the many differences between Margaret Vivian and her mother, Viola, there was one thing that they had in common: They both loved the outdoors. The forest, the fruit trees, the wild bougainvillea and myriad uncultivated flowers growing near the stream and high up in the mountains helped to soothe Margaret Vivian's soul and delivered her from the clutches of insanity – much in the same way they had been the boon of her mother, Viola's spirit.

However, since Margaret Vivian's going away to school, Viola had languished; alone and lonely, in her yard, she neither visited anyone in the village nor did she encourage visitors. Now, on Margaret Vivian's return, Viola behaved more than ever like her chickens; she remained cooped up in her house or in the yard all day and retired very early to her bed. Margaret Vivian, on the other hand, became the centre of her own narrative; her own story. She, who always believed that she was totally in control of her own destiny, spent hours – and sometimes days - ensconced in the bosom of the forest. There, she felt safe, for it was in the forest that her spirit and her soul were at peace.

Undisturbed and untroubled, she would lie back and think her own thoughts. It was there in the refuge of Nature, that Margaret Vivian came to the conclusion that for her, being alone did not translate into loneliness. At these times, her mind traveled into landscapes of her mind that were before unexplored, and unexamined. Ideas, some wild, some ingenious and some, very creative, filled her consciousness. These ideas nurtured her spirit; they allowed her to be her 'true' self. She realized that she did not need to concentrate on all those ideas that meandered through her mind, so she allowed them to float freely in her head and they were, like small pebbles in a stream, tossed about by the impetus of her thoughts, coming to rest where-ever they will. At such times, ensconced in the trees that gave her hungry soul life and protected physically from the glares of the sun by the shade of their overhanging branches, Margaret Vivian *was free.* Neither chained by causal laws nor tied to moral responsibility,

Margaret Vivian was free to be whatever she wanted. In the forest, there was no need to feel subservient or superior to any man or man-made laws – in the shape of her mother or the villagers. She could be herself – answerable only to Nature.

So Margaret Vivian's actions appeared frequently to be quite unpredictable to Viola - who did not know whether Margaret Vivian was going to shout or remain quiet - and in order to be at peace, Viola had reduced the enigma of Margaret Vivian to one idea that was easily explained and uncomplicated: Viola thought Margaret Vivian was a lunatic.

But Margaret Vivian was no lunatic. She thought of herself as strong willed and free; free to laugh or to cry, free to work or remain idle, free to love or to hate. She did not see herself as caught up in the conflicts of life and the ambivalence of mood nor was she troubled by the disconnections or the discontentment with life that so overwhelmed Viola. Margaret Vivian thought of herself as free from what could be termed 'the consciousness of necessity': of having to do, of having to be 'good'. And it was because of this way of looking at herself and at the world, that everyone whom she knew or knew about her, thought of her as 'dangerous' and an aberration.

Thinking her own thoughts, Viola sat on an old chair at the back of the henhouse. Nowadays that was as near as she got to the forest. She was weary – not only was she tired of the drudgery of her existence, but she was tired of the constant bickering and conflicts that were sparked at the slightest provocation between herself and Margaret Vivian. She told herself that, 'that girl had to go'. She could not tolerate living in the same house with Margaret Vivian anymore. The only time there had been peace was when Margaret Vivian was away, being educated at the convent school a few years ago. Now, there was some relief when she took herself off to the forest for a few days. And in some ways, Viola envied Margaret Vivian her freedom. She came and went as she pleased with no regard for her or for

Josephine. Viola thought that it must be great to do what you want, when you want, wherever you wanted to do it. But she knew life was not like that for almost all people. She surmised she fell into the group of the majority who was tied to conventions; who was in fact overcome by innumerable responsibilities.

Sighing heavily and looking wistfully towards the forest – the balm of her childhood, the home where all her dreams were formulated – and destroyed – she decided on the spur of the moment to take a walk once again into the bosom of that safe place; the sanctuary where, as a young child she had always felt the presence of a comforting force. She missed the wet smell of the earth, the shade of the large overhanging branches of the tall trees, the safety of the dark cavern-like places that beckoned her to come in and rest. All that, amplified by the silence of the forest, had always quieted her young excitable heart. The tranquility of Nature was her bane and her boon. The stillness of the forest had permitted the thinking of thoughts of which she would not have been able to imagine anywhere else. A smile appeared on her tired face as she walked towards the cocoa estate where her father loved to sit quietly under the trees and smoke the cigarettes her mother would not allow in the house. The coca estate was her father's favourite place and next to his cocoa estate, her father loved his cigarettes best. In the cocoa field, the earth exuded an unusual scent that reminded her of dogs and of squirrels; of the small animals of the forest with whom she always believed she had some kind of affinity. And the scent of her father's cigarettes, mixed with the wonderful smell of ripening cocoa had further increased its appeal.

As Viola walked into the bosom of the forest, it suddenly occurred to her, like a bolt from the blue, that maybe, just maybe, Margaret Vivian felt the same way about the wild and may now seek comfort in the belly of the forest. Like herself, maybe, the girl was greatly distressed by complicated relationships and found solace in the bosom of the natural world where the law of Nature was really survival of the fittest – without complications of personal attachments.

Almost without thinking, Viola was walking towards the stream where her life took that unfortunate turn so many years ago. As she approached the bank of the river, she looked up into the big chenette tree. The tree had grown old; its bark was gnarled, its large brown trunk looked ragged. Viola thought to herself that her beloved tree had grown as old and as worn as herself. But there was fruit on this tree. It would seem that the years of living were easier on this tree than on her.

As she walked, all the while looking up at the tree, she caught sight of Margaret Vivian. The girl was sleeping in the large Y between the old branches. She looked so vulnerable and so young. Her long frame was curled into a foetal position. One long arm hung loosely at her side, dropping way past her bent legs. The other was folded deep in her lap, but the forearm was positioned so that her wrist and long fingers were curled up under her chin. Only half of her face was visible from where Viola stood. Her small upturned nose seemed to be just a dot in her face. Her large lips were parted and two of her small white teeth protruded outwards. She had recently shaved off all of her thick black plaits that had lain down her back, always looking as though they were in a position of readiness to spring. Taut and tight, her plait had resembled a long coiled snake. Now, her head was almost bald, with tufts of hair just growing out of her scalp. Suddenly it occurred to Viola that Margaret Vivian looked just like Graham's mother. It was really strange that she had not paid much attention to the resemblance before. She was a beautiful girl. Her smooth black skin was shiny and glistened in the afternoon sun. She looked like what she was: a young black gazelle that was resting, but would be ready to leap at the slightest provocation.

As she looked up at this her first child, her heart cracked wide open with emotion and the resultant pain of knowledge and regret suffused her entire body. This girl spawned from the alcoholic heat of an ineffectual father and this child borne out of disgust and shame of an unaccommodating mother had, ironically enough, turned out to be the greatest love of Viola's life. It was a love that was both unspeakable and unspoken. This girl was her life, her love, her whole self. Viola could not comprehend the depths of this deep emotion. She had never felt what she experienced at this moment. As she looked up at her woe-begotten daughter, she knew without this girl, whether near to her or far from her - her life was incomplete. And the words flowed quickly and without effort into her bewildered mind. ... "There is no greater love than that in which He laid down his life for men". And then she remembered her mother, while talking to one of her friends, she had said to her that, "nobody *and I mean nobody,* should love anything or anyone like this. If you love anything or anyone more than the love of God, it would be taken from you".

I am the Lord thy God. There should be no other gods before me.

Viola became afraid. Unable to sustain such a surfeit of emotion, she lifted her arms to the tree that sheltered her child and then helplessly and hopelessly lowered her tired arms to her side. Why did they fight like banshees? Quickly lowering her gaze to the forest floor, Viola slowly walked on and sunk her tired body onto the sand of the river bank.

The river was very quiet. The water fled past quickly and soundlessly. It was as clear as day since no longer did many people wash their clothes or come to the river for water for their daily household tasks. Taking off her slippers, Viola placed her tired feet in the cool water. She swished her hand in the water, back and forth, back and forth, back and forth. The water swirled round and then continued its journey downstream. Viola's eyes followed the stream. The movement of the water and its steady flow brought back to her mind one of those poems that she had being taught as a child by Miss Cynthia, the village teacher. It was from Shakespeare's 'Hamlet". The children had to learn lines for the school play and she had learned hers quickly and well, because she wanted to play 'Ophelia'. But that was a very, very long time ago and she had not thought of anything as stirring as poetry for a long, long while. As she reminisced, she was quite surprised to realize that she remembered the entire poem - word for word:

There is a willow grows aslant a brook,
That shows his hoar leaves in the glassy stream;
There with fantastic garlands did she come,
Of crow-flowers, nettles, daisies and long purples,
That liberal shepherds give a grosser name,
But our cold maids do dead man's fingers call them:
There, on the pendent boughs her coronet weeds
Clambering to hang, an envious silver broke,
When down her weedy trophies and herself
Fell in the weeping brook. Her clothes spread wide,
And, Mermaid-like, awhile they bore her up...
Till that her garments, heavy with their drink,
Pull'd the poor wretch from her melodious lay
To muddy death..."

The poem was somewhat prophetic of her life. Viola thought of herself and her life and realized that she, unlike Ophelia, had not met a "muddy death", but she had had a murky life. Her spirit had drowned all those years ago in the stream of her life and she had become, because of it, a faceless, unrevealed creature; an innocent, destroyed by the machinations of Graham, her husband.

Thinking these piteous thoughts Viola was startled by the soft nasal voice behind her:

"Hello Mother."

Margaret Vivian had only called Viola 'Ma Ma' once and that was on the night of Graham's confession. To her, Viola was always 'Mother'. It sounded so cold and distant. However, she had always called her father 'Pa Pa'. At the sound of Margaret Vivian's voice, Viola turned around slowly. She was shocked by the animosity on Margaret Vivian's face. She had not heard her climb down from her perch in the chenette tree. She knew that this, her older daughter and herself were not friends, but the anger in Margaret Vivian's face told her that she had intruded in some way that was unforgivable. She did not want to think that her daughter saw her as The Enemy. There followed an uncomfortable silence, which was not helped by the rigid, uncompromising posture of the younger woman. Margaret Vivian stood before her mother, her long frame leaning against the trunk of the chenette tree. Viola raised herself slowly from the river bank and walked around her to an old rotten tree trunk which lay some way from the river. She smiled self-consciously, but Margaret either did not see the gesture or she ignored it. Sitting on the old trunk, Viola wanted to talk to her daughter. In some intuitive way, she knew that this was a good time to do so and there were some things in both their lives which needed attention. Maybe the quiet surroundings may calm Margaret Vivian ... and if she [Viola] did not raise her voice and did not appear to reproach her by word or gesture, they may be able to have some kind of conversation. But how was she to begin, how could she approach this daughter who stood before her like a lion ready to spring at its prey.

"We've got to talk, Margaret Vivian. I know you don't have much to say to me, but I believe that for us to live together in some kind of comfort, we will have to talk. We must say some things to each other. We cannot go on this way. Living like this is intolerable for me. Maybe it does not bother you, but it does me."

"Then what do you want to say?"

Viola shifted her position

"I don't know. I want to talk. ... but I don't know.........."

Margaret Vivian interrupted her mother's answer by turning her back and walking away from her. She turned around a little distance away.

"You don't know WHAT?? You always seemed to know everything."

Margaret's retort was full of venom. Sometimes she did not understand why her mother got her so angry. All Viola had to do was to look at Margaret Vivian and she felt all sanity leave her. Margaret Vivian suffered a deep pain in her head and a sudden lurch of her heart. She wanted to hurt her mother. She herself did not understand this overwhelming hate. At that moment, she truly wished Viola would drop dead in front of her – for her to see, for her to witness her being obliterated from the world and from her sight. To lessen this uncontrollable anger, which, somewhere in the back of her mind, she knew was out of all proportion to the situation and to give herself time to repress these emotions, Margaret Vivian pulled her short loose shirt tightly around her slim frame as though to protect herself from some wild, unmanageable force and then she exclaimed:

"You believe you know how to deal with everything. Well, let me tell you lady, I know a few things of my own. I know that you hated looking at me when I was very young. I know that you killed Pa Pa with your whining and your self-righteous behaviour. Maybe Josephine is afraid to confront you, but I am not. I know how Pa Pa felt all his life: lost, ignored, lonely, afraid that at any moment, you will tell everyone about his 'sin' against you. You see, I <u>know</u> where I was conceived!! Was it right here? Is it why you have returned to the forest after all these years?"

Viola stood upright at this last retort. Her head began to spin. For a moment, she though she had misunderstood what Margaret Vivian had said. Did she say she *knew* how she was conceived? Margaret Vivian *knew*. She had never told *anyone* about *that* matter. Then, what was Margaret Vivian saying? *She could not know!* Viola stared at her daughter wide eyed. The vehemence with which Margaret Vivian had revealed her knowledge told Viola that she was speaking the truth. No one could state anything with so much emotion – so violently – unless it was true.

"What... what are you saying?" Viola stammered.

For a long, long while the two women stared at each other. Their eyes were locked in a fierce embrace. They did not seem to be mother and daughter, but more like hunter and prey - and Viola had nowhere to hide; she was vulnerable; lost confused, unable to fathom the idea that her daughter knew of her misfortune. How did she find out? Bewildered, she lowered her tired body on to the old rotten log, afraid to ask the necessary question.

Sensing her mother's dismay and confusion, and relishing the pleasure that she got from it, Margaret Vivian told Viola how she knew; that as a child, she had inadvertently overheard her mother and Graham's conversation; that her father was a rapist. And later she realized that her mother was a self-indulgent, self-righteous, detestable woman who used her silence as a weapon. Margaret Vivian took pleasure in rupturing again the wound of pain that she knew her mother suffered; the disappointment, the betrayal that she experienced, when she discovered her father's treachery. What she did not say to Viola was the pain that *she* had suffered all these long years and how it had affected the way *she* thought - not only about Viola or Graham - but how it influenced the way she dealt with other people; strangers, her friends at school - and especially, her sister, Josephine.

Josephine was always the innocent. She ignored every difficult situation. Sensitive and compliant, she acquiesced to every request of both her parents. To her, to keep the peace was paramount. It did not matter that there were so many other levels of discord and distress surrounding her. Josephine lived in her own bubble, an unreal world that protected her from the vagaries of disharmony and discomfort. It was because of Josephine's docility that Margaret Vivian was compelled to protect the submissive younger sister from the domination of a harsh, oppressive mother. But then, where was Margaret Vivian's home, her heart[h], her place of solace? Who was to protect Margaret Vivian? How does one measure absence?

For Viola, the forest was both blight and blessing and there was no happy way to leave the forest again. No tears flowed after the accusations spat out by Margaret Vivian. In truth, she was never a woman to cry. She was never a teary-eyed woman who seemed to get relief from shedding tears, so she reverted to her old defense: She remained silent. Not a word escaped her lips. Slowly and with a heavy ache in her heart, she walked out of the only place that had given her joy and back to her home.

And Margaret Vivian, after the pain and hurt she had inflicted on her mother, in a place where she herself had always found solace, felt no pleasure. This was no victory: This trashing of the other brought no triumph. All she felt was sadness and a deep, deep pain in the pit of her stomach. She could not return to that place that was never home really. She had no home. She felt safe nowhere.

At least Josephine seemed happy; her other worldly nature shielded her from the ravages of the mind and the torment of the spirit. Margaret Vivian had no such protection. So for a long while after her mother had silently walked out of the forest and away from her, she sat on the dark, wet brown earth. Then she got up quickly, walked to the stream and allowed her body to be submerged in the cold, cold water - just as her mother had done so long ago. Her hand trailed in the cold, cold water; back and forth, back and forth, back and forth. Then she washed her face in the cool stream of water. She felt the clear liquid flow over the front of her thin blouse so that she experienced the sensation of wetness, like the sudden thrill of baptism. In all this time, no wild thoughts filled her mind, but she did think of people and far away places - and anonymity. Then she rose out of the water and walked out of the forest – in the opposite direction to that of her mother.

EIGHT

Margaret Vivian

*My spirits were elevated by the enchanting appearance of nature; the past
was blotted from my memory, the present was tranquil, and the future
gilded by bright rays of hope and anticipations of joy.*

Mary Shelley

EIGHT

On leaving the forest that day, after the terrible row with her mother, Margaret Vivian had walked to the small town of Wilton where she intended to overnight at her uncle's home on the pretense of visiting her grandmother, Vivian. She hoped to taxi into town the next morning. That was as far as she had planned. Ironically, it was lucky for her that at this time, Vivian's health had deteriorated physically and she was unable to do much for herself, therefore she was glad to have one of her own close by to look after her needs. As a result, Margaret Vivian's arrival was opportune and to everyone's surprise, she turned out to be a wonderful companion and a good nurse for her grandmother. Both her uncle and aunt were relieved at this astonishing side of Margaret Vivian's personality because they had always believed that all she was, was a wretch and a troublemaker; an aberration and a lunatic.

Vivian stayed with her grandmother for two years and three months and dedicated herself entirely to her welfare until her death, when Vivian passed away without fuss or drama on a cold November night. In all that time, Margaret Vivian had glimpsed her own mother on two occasions of the many times Viola visited her mother. Margaret Vivian never stayed around when Viola came to town. Viola had wanted her mother back with her in the country, and Vivian wanted to return to her husband's house. However, she was aware that if she returned to her home, where she would have liked to have lived out her last days, Margaret Vivian would be at loose ends, because it was impossible in Margaret Vivian's way of thinking that she could *ever* enter her mother's house again. So Vivian sacrificed her last desire for the security and comfort of her old home for the safe keeping and happiness of her first grandchild.

On the first anniversary of her grandmother's death, when her grief had mellowed and her restlessness threatened to rear its edgy head once more, Margaret Vivian had picked herself up one rainy morning and with only the clothes on her back and a change of underclothing in her bag, she left her uncle's home. There were no teary goodbyes, no regrets, and if her uncle's wife had known she was leaving, there would have been only relief. She moved to the main city which was approximately four hundred and twenty five miles away from her mother. She had stayed two nights at her old school friend Yvonne, who had told her, in no uncertain terms, that her stay could not be extended. Yvonne lived near the main city with her husband and two small children in a small apartment. She could walk to her job, which was as an accountant in one of the better establishments. Her two girls aged six and four, were timid, shy children, who Margaret Vivian thought to herself had an uncanny resemblance to Yvonne's husband, Samuel. He was a big, burly fellow who worked in a small construction company as a building supervisor. On meeting, both Margaret Vivian and Samuel had taken an immediate dislike to each other. It could have been that Margaret Vivian, on seeing this tall, huge man, had reflected on the many girlish and romantic conversations she and Yvonne had had about a choice of mate, and Samuel was the exact opposite of Yvonne's dream. Or it could have been that on meeting Samuel, Margaret Vivian was unable to conceal her disappointment, and Samuel was astute enough to perceive her surprise and obvious disappointment. Not only did Samuel resemble an overgrown rugby player but he had an ego to match his size. He had convinced himself that he was God's gift to women, especially to Yvonne, and she in turn fed his delusion. Such disappointment and antagonism which Samuel perceived exuded from Margaret Vivian could not be tolerated in his home. And since *his wife* was quite satisfied with *her life*, he was not going to let any such nuisance, such as Margaret Vivian, threaten the peaceful arrangement of hierarchy in his house. Margaret could not stay and that was that.

It was ten years after her rejection of Samuel and his dismissal of her. The thirty five year old Margaret Vivian was doing well for herself. The first three years after the death of Vivian, her beloved grandmother, were hard years. Margaret Vivian had lived at many different places; she stayed at old people's home for months and looked after these old women for a while so that she could get shelter and money to buy food and to save. She also spent weeks in one room apartments that were located in places where the people were crude and crass and the surroundings filthy, but the rooms were cheap....

And then she lived for years with Stanley, whose second wife had left him on hearing of his liaison with a woman whom she told everyone had no real looks and no class and was as black as coal to boot.

Margaret Vivian was always very ambitious and when she met Stanley she realized that it was possible to be rich, well-informed *and* independent. During the years before she met Stanley at the race track, where she usually went to relax on Sunday mornings, she had carved out in her head the way she wanted her life to run. She knew she could not be the loving, caring wife and attentive mother as her grandmother. Under no circumstances did she want to be anything like her self-righteous, opinionated, suffering mother. And she would prefer to die than be like the soft, yielding woman as her younger sister was. She wanted to be a success, but she was having difficulty in defining what that meant. Although the pull of money was not magnetic, she knew by now that in reality, it was necessary for successful living, so Margaret Vivian had returned to school. She knew she was smart and she knew she would be able to do the work, but studying at the university was hard and after working all day, the nights seemed long and tiring. In addition, early into her first semester, Margaret Vivian realized she could not pass her examinations in the way she did at the convent; by insulting the other girls, being disrespectful to all the nuns, except Sister Marie Rose and reading enough just to cover the material taught. However, before her impetus for studying could wane, she met Stanley, who helped her to re-define the meaning of success.

Stanley was an expatriate who had come to the country to work off shore and to experience the type of climate he had always craved. Born in Belgium and raised by parents who traveled the world for fun and excitement, they had finally settled in the United States long enough to give him a good, sound education. He had always loved Geography and had inherited from his parents the gene of constant movement, constant change. At twenty five, he had met his first wife, Dorothy, in Texas, where he had studied. She, a woman of means and eight years his senior, had borne him two children, who were now grown and independent. He divorced her in Venice on one of their many trips there, where Dorothy had hoped to rekindle their dying romance. Stanley did not return to the States after this unhappy divorce, but instead, took a plane to Jamaica where he lay in the sun and worked, in that order, for about five years. Then he moved to the island of Taringa.

At the time when Margaret Vivian met Stanley, he was a middle-aged man who realized that he was on the other side of the mountain of life and the way downhill could be fast and furious. Stanley was now bored with his second wife, a young woman about Margaret Vivian's age who had convinced herself that she had caught a meal ticket for her life, one which should – with luck - extend beyond her husband's by many years. Unfortunately for her, after the initial excitement of marrying, the novelty of the opportunist had worn off and Stanley was bored. He was ready to move on. And then he saw Margaret Vivian.

Margaret Vivian had left that Sunday morning in all the rain to go to the racetrack. She told herself that the weather would not deprive her of her only means of enjoyment. She had left home very early because she wanted to get a good vantage point. In addition, arriving early at the race track allowed her the luxury of settling nearby without being too close to the excitement or to be uncomfortable because all the flying dust, the dirt and noise. She was lucky enough to get some space under the almond trees situated on a small incline quite close to the horse's track and this vantage point allowed for a breathtaking view of the horses as they came galloping around the corner and as they sprinted down the track to the finish line. Margaret Vivian visualised the culmination of the races: It was the final phase that delighted her most. These beautiful animals, their skins glistening with sweat, their royal heads raised to the sky, eyes opened wide, nostrils trembling from the exertion and their long, lean, graceful bodies alert to every change in the tense atmosphere. The images excited her. These beautiful creatures were not in the race for the cash prize. Their focus was the sheer joy of the contest, the challenge, the exuberance of speed.

Margaret Vivian was excited. Anticipation of the races was making her restless. Leaving her chosen position, she walked across the track to the small lily pond and stood watching the small fishes as they swam around in their small dirty pool. She made a remarkable picture leaning against the rail, meant to keep children out of danger. She was dressed in a short, black and white polka dot dress that was about five inches above her knees. Around her waist was a red pleated velvet band, also about five inches wide. This band was tied in a bow, in school girl fashion - at the back, and the ends of the bow drooped down to the back of her knees. She was bare legged and on her feet was a pair of white leather sandals with very high heels. Where the two thin straps intersected on her sandals, she had placed two large bows in the same polka dot fabric as her dress. As she moved, the bows on her feet moved and so did the wide - rimmed white straw hat that covered her small head. Her long plait of hair which usually lay flat against her back moved in tandem with the hat. Margaret Vivian looked like an overgrown school girl in wide sun glasses.

Stanley, walking across from his perch in the public stands to be closer to the race track and to be rid of the loud ruckus from the many noisy people in the stands, caught sight of Margaret Vivian. He was intrigued by her unusual appearance as she stood alone near the fish pond. She did present a startling figure in polka dots as she leaned forward peering into the pond. Her legs were long and lean and her posture suggested a graceful polka dot gazelle. The sun had just appeared after the early morning downpour and its weak rays were diffused under the cloudy sky, so Stanley, unable to see very clearly and unable to contain his curiosity about the unusual image of Margaret Vivian, walked across to her and remarked;

"I guess it is cooler out here near the fish pond."

Margaret Vivian did not respond and Stanley, taking her disregard of him as some sort of mating game, insisted that she acknowledge his presence, so he began to whistle - off key. He continued for about five minutes, before he realized that Margaret Vivian was not deliberately ignoring his intrusion, but she was really absorbed in what she was observing. Abruptly, he stopped whistling and very seriously asked;

"Are you alone at the race track? Well, so am I."

His sudden change in tone and demeanor caught Margaret Vivian's attention and she looked around. Stanley was immediately struck by her wide, dark, intelligent eyes and her serious look. He had expected something quite different – maybe a coquettish young girl who was out for a day of fun and attention. Margaret Vivian did not seem as young as he had thought and he was taken aback by her serious gaze: she looked at him straight in the eyes and did not blink. In turn, Margaret Vivian was intrigued by Stanley's unusual looks; his hair was dark brown and long and held back in a pony tail. His light blue eyes were crinkled at the corners as he smiled at her and his mouth, a bit off center was open in a wide smile. He was very tall and very, very thin with long arms that seem almost to touch the ground. His arms appeared to be disproportionate to his body, but somehow he did not look awry. It is true that he was unusual looking and it was his odd looks that caught her fancy. So, smiling at him, she answered;

85

"Hey!!"

The light high musical tones of the monosyllabic response captivated Stanley further and he came a bit closer to her. They were two unusual looking people, who, although they made an unlikely couple physically, would realize that they were in tune intellectually. It was the beginning of a friendship and a love affair that was to last a decade.

On returning to her apartment in town after the races, Margaret Vivian was feeling in a good mood. She and Stanley had had the most invigorated discussions about everything and anything. It was the first time in Margaret Vivian's life that she had felt so enervated and so alive. She always knew that she had this enormous capacity to talk and talk and talk, in the same way that she was able to create images, to draw pictures in her mind's eye.

Now, serving as a facilitating force, Stanley triggered Margaret Vivian's enormous verbal capacity in a positive way and she was able to express her ideas with the easy facility of someone whose purpose on this earth was 'to invent' through the magic of words. In the company of Stanley, words flowed out of her, like a cool shower of rain that refreshed and clarified her ideas while cleansing her spirit of doubt of self and dread of her mother.

Before, when she spoke to or about her mother, her words had seemed to develop a life of their own; they became a torrent, a violent flow of expressions, a deluge of words that were aggressive in intent and abusive in nature. At those times what she had said stung and hurt people at whom they were directed. Her stream of abuse was a malignant force that impelled others to hit back and hurt in return. And because of such exchanges, Margaret Vivian suffered the pain and humiliation of condemnation and sometimes unfair criticism.

In retrospect, it is easy to surmise that it was mainly because of this unfortunate 'gift' that her mother and herself had experienced so much heartache and so much pain from each other. She had hurled words at her mother like people had hurled stones at 'the sinful woman' – and in the end, it was she, Margaret Vivian, who felt crucified and Viola who remained silent, sullen and sanctimonious.

The years with Stanley tempered Margaret Vivian's verbal rage and cooled her sulphurous nature. She forgot, for months at a time, the pain she had felt. Stanley became her love, her spiritual mentor; her saviour.

NINE

Margaret Vivian and Stanley

Love is no hot-house flower, but a wild plant, born of a wet night, born of an hour of sunshine; sprung from wild seed, blown along the road by a wild wind. A wild plant that, when it blooms by chance within the hedge of our gardens, we call a flower; and when it blooms outside we call a weed; but, flower or weed, whose scent and colour are always, wild!

John Galsworthy The Forsyte Saga

NINE

It was the best years of Margaret Vivian's life. She exulted in the intellectual stimulation that Stanley's presence facilitated and she enjoyed the entertainment that his wealth so graciously allowed. And Stanley, completely enamoured by the unconventional and somewhat eccentric Margaret Vivian, settled comfortably and happily for the first time in his adult life. Never had Stanley met any woman who was so unaware of the potency of her appeal and because Margaret Vivian was so oblivious of this attraction, she behaved in unselfconscious ways that increased Stanley's fascination with her. It was ironic that Stanley's way of thinking about Margaret Vivian was the opposite of what almost everybody else, including her family, thought about her: Stanley believed that she was wonderful and therefore, for the first time in her life, Margaret Vivian felt a positive pull and power towards someone else. This magnetism was for her extremely exciting and was increased by the fact that it came from a person of the opposite sex. She was intrigued by Stanley's response and reaction to herself. Since she had never experienced any lasting love affairs with boys - or men - this love affair aroused within her a curiosity and a deep fascination. Before, she had always been satisfied by her egocentric self and her kinship with Nature and had searched no further for any other kind of spiritual connection or affection. As a result, Margaret Vivian did not, at first, interpret this attraction to Stanley as a lure of love. She really did not know what that meant in the conventional sense. What she did know though, was that for the first time in her entire life, she felt as happy and as comfortable with another person as she did when, as a child, she had escaped from her miserable world and into the bosom of the forest.

What other people thought of Stanley and Margaret Vivian's relationship was another matter. Many people viewed these two people as the most unusual couple. However, Stanley was not bothered by what other people thought and Margaret Vivian had never paid any attention to the thinking of others. Consequently, they experienced life in a world in which they both ignored, overlooked disregarded the opinion of others. In other words, they lived their lives unencumbered by the capriciousness and cynicism of others. Thus, their relationship took on an aspect that was particularly childlike; it was trusting and uncomplicated. Pure and simple, this was a human connection that was ingenuous; frank, honest and enjoyable.

For many years – eight to be exact – Margaret Vivian and Stanley behaved as though the world revolved around them. They made it their own. They created a haven out of their feelings for each other and shared their enjoyment through visiting and seeing and experiencing other ways of living and other ways of life. Cosseted and protected by Stanley's wealth, their lives became a wonder, particularly for Margaret Vivian, who in all her thirty five years had never left the shores of Taringa.

On her first visit to Europe, Margaret Vivian was awestruck by the architecture of Rome – particularly St. Peter's. As she entered the church alone, she could understand why Sister Sarah Rose seemed overwhelmed as she related stories to her young students at the convent school of the magnificence of Michelangelo and the purity of his art. However, Margaret Vivian's own likeness for the great Florentine artist went beyond his work. As she read about the artist's independence, his persistence in his work and his determination, she was guided by his elevated ideals, his love for his art and his passion for his religion. This was an obsession that she understood, for it matched the fertility of her own mind and her passion for Nature.

On this, her first visit to The Pieta in the French Chapel at St. Peter's, Margaret Vivian stood before the figure completely absorbed. It was at this time that she remembered her own puerile prank at school when she covered the Virgin Mary in her grandmother's medication. Now, she felt sorrow – an emotion that was heavier than the righteous anger of Sister Anne Marie at her [Margaret Vivian's] desecration. As she moved up the aisle of the church, Margaret Vivian was unaware of the people around her. Her entire body and mind were centred on the beauty of the Cathedral which was enveloped in an ethereal light. In the magnificence of such Presence, she encountered a divine greatness, but also experienced an exalted grief that reminded her of her own mother.

On her second visit to The Pieta, this time in the company of Stanley, Margaret Vivian could only think of her parents; of their lives, tormented and long suffering. She relived her father's death and her mother's enduring pain. For Margaret Vivian, these two journeys to Rome came to represent pilgrimages to an altar of remembrance when her now stable and lasting love for Stanley aided her in an understanding of other people's human frailty - especially the suffering of her mother.

Later that week, as she stood before the painting of the Mona Lisa and stared back defiantly, at the piercing look of the woman in the painting, there was created a moment surreal: She felt her own eyes turning inward, examining her own self, her own life, her own truth. She was astounded by this clarity and wandered off in a daze where later Stanley found her sitting on the steps of the Sacre Coeur rocking back and forth, back and forth, back and forth as she was wont to do.

To calm her turbulent spirit, Stanley took Margaret Vivian on a memorable visit to the centre of Paris at night. This vibrant city stirred within her all the enthusiasm and romanticism that marked her approach to life. Enarmoured of its scintillating excitement, thrilled by its succulent food and wines, she was captivated by the city's level of sophistication and immersed herself in it. Like a child at the circus, Margaret Vivian luxuriated in an old world in which to her, everything was new.

I have never felt so pained and so happy at the same time. I am enchanted with the vivacity and passion of this city, I am humbled by my experiences at St. Peter's and now, I believe I am becoming enlightened as to the twists and turns of the human psyche. My mother.... What does she want, what did she want from my father? So much to learn.....

Such a beautiful, tragic developed world in which the manifestations of itself is so closely replicated in nature: Shape and Structure, Figure and Form, Death and Life, Birth and Renewal, Sin and Forgiveness, Happiness and Misery, all these concepts, ideas and ideals combine, mingle, blend together, drift apart to create unique experiences for every individual.

Really, we live in a world within a world, within a world - Nature, culture, relationships, - all of us belong in a complicated world where its axis – as psychological balance as well as disequilibrium – is forever spinning but also whirling forward, generating movements that catapult us further into the unknown and thereby fashion a life for us that is both exciting and fearful. Our world takes us back and forth, back and forth, back and forth, swinging from the vicissitudes of reality into the charmed world of dreams and imaginings and back to the world of memory .....

Much of Margaret Vivian's new way of perceiving life was due to the enormous influence of Stanley. He was her anchor, her reliable hour hand. She was the minute hand of Time, moving faster and sometimes erratically and idiosyncratically and responding always, to her own beat - or tick as it were

---

It was on their return to Taringa, when Margaret Vivian was awakened suddenly one November morning by Stanley's groans of discomfort. She was alarmed. To her knowledge, Stanley was never sick. Always the strong, healthy man, she believed that he had led a charmed life in which sickness had played no part.

Stanley, unwilling to alarm Margaret Vivian, had pretended that the pains were not as bad as they really were. He did not tell her that after their last visit overseas, the pains were getting worse.

Immediately on his return home, he had decided that he would visit his doctor. The next morning after his return, Stanley had showered quickly, dressed and left the house. He travelled all the way to the small town of Wilton to see his friend who was also his doctor. He had also experienced numerous dizzy spells and even before that, he had continually felt nagging pains all over his body. Although his appetite had not decreased, he had recently begun to lose a lot of weight and had developed a persistent cough. To Margaret Vivian's numerous and anxious enquiries after his health, he had jokingly remarked that he had decided that getting older was hazardous to one's health and he needed to streamline his body to cope with the physical onslaught, so he had decided to lose some weight. They both laughed heartily at his statement; Stanley because it relieved Margaret Vivian of some anxiety about himself and Margaret Vivian because she believed that Stanley would not lie to her about important matters.

This time Stanley's visit with the doctor took a serious turn. He was mandated to take a series of blood tests and to have some X-rays done. Surprisingly enough, even to his medical friend, Stanley did not seem surprised at the request, and neither did he appear upset. In the doctor's experience, many of his patients were visibly upset at the requests and usually asked many questions. Stanley asked no questions. It seemed almost as though he knew what was going to be found. Quickly he left the doctor's office and returned home.

It was two weeks before the results would come in. Stanley had returned from the doctor's and had behaved in his usual carefree manner. Never for a moment did he appear worried, but he had refused to discuss any of this matter with Margaret Vivian. When she asked about his visit to the doctor, he said that he was fine. She left him alone. Stanley had always been very silent on matters relating to his health and she did not want to appear to be a nag – like her mother.

The results of his blood tests were positive, as he had suspected they would have been. Stanley had contracted H.I.V. He knew that the relationship between himself and Margaret Vivian had been trustworthy and therefore he believed that this tragic and overwhelming situation had its genesis in times before the beginning of their relationship. It wasn't her fault. He knew that. He was afraid. To suspect that you have contracted a serious communicable disease is one thing. To have it confirmed – without doubt – by a trusted medical authority was another. Stanley knew that the disease could be treated but his illness seemed to have progressed rapidly in a very short period of time. He could hardly stand the sudden darts of excruciating pain up his back. The soreness in his knees made it difficult for him to walk sometimes and the tenderness of his gums made the chewing of his food as well as swallowing difficult. But the worse pain was the pain in his heart, the ache he experienced knowing that what he was living through would end his life. It was terminal. He would have to leave Margaret Vivian. He did not know what to say to her, what would she think, what would she do? He had kept this vital information a secret from his mate who, by now, more than likely, had contracted the dread disease herself. How should he plan the rest of his life? But most importantly for Stanley, he did not know how he would tell Margaret Vivian. So he waited and waited and waited........

Then, she found out.

Margaret Vivian was going through the papers to plan for their next trip, which was a short holiday to Grenada where they hoped to visit the wonderful spice gardens and swim in the extraordinarily beautiful peaceful waters around Gran Anse. She felt a bit disappointed at the lack of enthusiasm Stanley exhibited for the long awaited trip. She knew he was not himself lately. He seemed worried about something. Any enquiry on her part upset him further so she kept silent and watched and waited. She knew that the trip to Grenada would cheer him up – make him return to his outlandish, boyish nature. For her, the trip represented a wonder. She was all excited to be in the forest and mountains of Grenada. She imagined it to be as beautiful as the forest near her home at Southwood. She missed the trees, the soothing waters, the peacefulness and serenity of the woods. She could not wait.

And on searching for their passports, she found the medical reports. At first she did not believe it. Peering shortsightedly at the papers, she checked the name, the address and then the name again. She told herself that it could not be true. Not her Stanley. Not Stanley. He would tell her. He would not hide this from her. It was too important. It was life shattering. Her own words of a shattered life brought a smile to her lips and she thought if it wasn't so serious, the language would be funny. But it was serious, it was real. This was not funny. She sat on the bed and her life – her whole life - her early life flashed before her. She remembered her mother. She recalled her father. He was crying and asking forgiveness of her mother for not having told her his most awful secret about the rape. All the while she had hid under their bed. Was it that when things hurt too much, so much, it could not be articulated: It had to remain unsaid? Was that why Stanley had become so silent? Somehow, she felt no animosity, no hate, no rage towards Stanley. How did she, all of a sudden, understand this level of treachery? Was it because now that she found herself in the position of being betrayed – like her mother - by someone that you love, that she could comprehend the turmoil of the loved one's transgressions, their weaknesses, their pain? Margaret Vivian sighed loudly. No tears came. No anger. She felt numb and then she thought of Stanley - dying. Her own imminent death did not occur to her, not then – not yet.

Such a beautiful world. To leave it is sad. To leave the sun, the sky, the forest, the trees, the fruits, the flowers, the weeds, the rain, the rivers, the seas .... and the ones that you love.

What will I do when Stanley is gone, how will I cope? Is this what loss is? Is this numb sensation of nothingness what loss is? Loss of one's mate, loss of one's love? Loss of one's family? Loss of one's innocence?

My mother had her innocence taken away from her. Is this what it felt like? A void that cannot be filled, a hole that holds no water, a weight that has no mass, a room without air, a language without words; still, silent, soundless, voiceless, wordless, unspeaking and unspeakable – unsaid.

Margaret Vivian sat on her bed, her head bowed low and her long, gangly arms hanging down between her legs. She realized that if this was what loss was; an existential nothingness that deprived you of everything and everyone, then this was hell - a world where you are alone and apart from all for whom you care. For her, this was *beyond* hell. It was an excruciatingly painful thing in which existence dissolved into nothingness. She thought:

"My mother ... myself. ... Stanley."

Such devastation she could not stomach, so she vomited all over the clean, new sheet on the bed and the loud retching, brought Stanley running into the room. His first reaction was one of concern, until he saw the medical report in Margaret Vivian's hand. He stepped back. Stood still. Then slowly he raised his head. His blue watery eyes collided with the pain in Margaret Vivian's. She knew. There was no need to tell. Kneeling beside the weeping woman, Stanley attempted to comfort her and together, they sat on the soft bed and rocked back and forth, back and forth, back and forth. It was ironic. It was like the murderer comforting the mourner. But in this situation, there was no accuser, no judge – judgment was suspended, maybe ... maybe to be brought up in another time and at another place.

Margaret Vivian and Stanley did not make the longed-for trip to Grenada, but instead, they visited Margaret Vivian's family in Southwood. It was at Margaret Vivian's suggestion and Stanley was pleased that at last she was making some attempt to heal the large abyss that separated her from her family. After all these long years; with no contact, no correspondence, Margaret had recently begun sending her mother short notes that were really small talk. When her mother responded to these tentative attempts at reconciliation, Margaret Vivian was glad. Then they began to talk on the phone – for short periods, because Viola did not like the telephone much. It was during these short conversations that Margaret Vivian learned of the premature death of her younger sister Josephine - in childbirth and of the existence of her young daughter, her niece Olivia, who was being cared for by Viola. Margaret thought that it was ironic that her grandmother, Vivian, had to look after her because of the trauma of her own mother's experience, and now her mother, Viola was doing the same for her niece, Olivia. Margaret Vivian also learned that her younger brother who had lived in town for some time, had moved back home with his wife to help with the farm, but they had eventually migrated to the United States. They had no children. Her older brother Mark, still lived at home with his mother, still farmed the land and was still unmarried.

Stanley was also happy to know that on his passing Margaret Vivian could return to the embrace of her family. She was the prodigal daughter and he knew that her 'second coming' will excite the curiosity of many of the villagers. In order to experience their reconciliation privately and quietly, both Viola and Margaret Vivian agreed that she should return a day or two earlier than was made known to the entire village.

Viola was happy to see her long lost child. Her first reaction was one of great pride, because Margaret Vivian looked so well and so prosperous too. She looked like something out of one of those magazines her father used to bring to her on his visits to town so many years ago. Margaret Vivian wore a loose yellow frock that fell from her shoulders to her knees in one smooth flow. Her dress was of soft cotton that looked as though it had just been ironed. She had tied a yellow ribbon to match around her big, straw hat. [These large straw hats had become Margaret Vivian's signature] and her many bracelets jangled as she moved her hands up and down. Viola's second reaction to her daughter's arrival was one of sorrow. Viola felt sad that she had missed so many of Margaret Vivian's youthful years. At close range Margaret Vivian was no longer a very young woman. If Viola could remember correctly, she would be close to forty. Forty years old! She marveled at the many years that had gone by. She had missed some very important milestones in her daughter's life. She missed her turning twenty and the youthful exuberance and enthusiasm that a twenty year old possessed. She missed her turning thirty when the accompanying sobriety of responsibility and temperance and self-control took hold. However, she was happy to see her before she, somewhat over fifty, passed on.

Margaret Vivian on the other hand was shocked at the appearance of her mother. As she counted the years, she realized that her mother was close to sixty years old. However, she looked like a very old woman. Viola's hair had gone completely grey and she wore it in a tight bun at the top of her head. Her body sagged; her arms were loose, her neck folded and her stomach drooped in a faded cotton dress that hung loosely around her aging body. . Margaret Vivian felt guilty that so many years had intervened, so many milestones in the family had been missed; so many birthdays of people in her family and in her village, so many births, that of her niece and of her village friends' children, so many deaths - of her sister and older people in the village. A lifetime had elapsed. The changes were many. It was sad but life stands still for no one.

And then her mother smiled. Margaret Vivian had never been accustomed to seeing her mother smile and on the rare occasion when she had done so, it had changed her entire countenance and amazed the young girl. The same thing happened now. Viola was always a very beautiful girl and a smile always changed her expression from mere beauty to a luminescent loveliness. And this miracle happened once more. Her big black eyes, so much like Margaret Vivian and Josephine's, opened wide and her small, up-tilted nose turned upwards further, so that her cheeks seem to expand and then plummet into the depths of their dimples. Her full lips turned up at the corners and opened ever so slowly to reveal the small perfect white teeth that Margaret Vivian remembered so well. Stanley was stunned at the change in Viola's appearance, but Margaret Vivian only looked at her mother because as she smiled this time, even the aura around her was transformed. Viola smile exuded welcome; it was the forgiveness that had remained unspoken and it told of an understanding that remained unsaid.

And there was Olivia. The child – she seemed about twelve years old. She stood very close to her grandmother, hugging her arm. She was a seemingly quiet child who resembled her mother Josephine, not only in looks, but it seemed also in temperament. She looked fearfully at her long lost aunt and at her companion and would have run off if these visitors had come too close to her. So Margaret Vivian did not rush up to her mother and hug her the way she would have liked to do. That was not the way they greeted each other. She waited.

After a short while of staring at Margaret Vivian, Olivia ran off on to the verandah of the house and Vivian took the opportunity to clasp her mother in her arms. At first, Viola was stiff; the welcome was so unexpected and unaccustomed. Then, her body unbending, she released all the pent up maternal love that she had harboured so quietly and intensely for this woman. But she did not cry. Viola never cried. However, she felt her muscles relax; her body softened and her arms yielded up and enfolded Margaret Vivian. She forgot their misunderstandings, the hurt and the pain that marked their former relationship. It was like the rain had fallen and the river had overflowed its bank, softening the hard, dry earth after a season of drought.

After the intensity of the greeting, Margaret Vivian introduced the two people whom she loved most – Viola and Stanley. Her mother walked ahead of them into the house. It was just as she had remembered it. The wooden verandah seemed to have been repaired in a few places, but the wooden floor looked as sturdy as ever. The banisters seemed to be of new wood and they were painted in a bright green.

The house was the same. There were plants everywhere; ferns hung from the ceiling of the verandah, bougainvillea of every hue; red and white and yellow, grew against the walls of the house and peeped over the window sill. There were orchids hanging on the cool side of the house near the kitchen, palms decorated every corner of the house and right near the steps, just outside the kitchen was her mother's beautiful and scented garden; lemon grass, and thyme and rosemary, parsley and chives.

In one corner of the verandah stood the old rocking chair. It looked the same, except that the cane of the seating was changed and there was a pillow with Viola's embroidery of a sunflower placed carefully on the seat. Quickly, Margaret Vivian sat on the chair and suddenly, it moved forward. She sat there and rocked back and forth, back and forth, back and forth and the old chair creaked under her weight.

Then getting up off the rocking chair, Margaret Vivian entered the drawing room. She parted the curtains at the door and the memories of her young life floated before her. In the living room stood the old wooden morris chairs - with new covers. The teak dining table and six chairs were in their usual place in the corner near the kitchen. Then near the kitchen entrance, stood the safe, where her mother placed all her good dishes and where Margaret Vivian had stood, pained and grieving and shocked as she realized that her Pa Pa had died.

Charging into her own bedroom, she saw that it had been overtaken by Olivia. There were clothes and books everywhere. But her bed was the same and so was the cane basket that held her precious under things. Margaret Vivian stood for a long while, taking in the smell and scent of the room. It smelled just as it did all those years ago.

For nearly two years, Margaret Vivian and Stanley, after building a small house deep in the forest, lived a wonderful life. For Margaret

Vivian, it was like heaven. She had everything she desired; Stanley, the closeness of nature and her family. The small wooden house looked as though it was part of the forest. Very much like a tree house, it stood on tall stilts dug deep into the earth and secured also by the huge branches of surrounding trees. They had done a wonderful job with the help of Jordan, the carpenter and her Uncle Mark. The birds of the forest mistakenly took it for part of the forest and flew through and around it, attesting to its 'naturalness'.

And then things changed. Stanley got very sick. Margaret Vivian spent days and nights without sleep. She never left Stanley in the care of anyone; not her mother, Viola or her niece, Olivia or any stranger. She looked after him with the same ferocity and love that she had administered care to her grandmother, Vivian. But the effort took its toll. She became exhausted from lack of sleep and grew tired of the torment of watching Stanley suffer.

Stanley could not breathe. His chest heaved again and again with every painful breath. His face was contorted. Most of his teeth had fallen out and his gums were always sore. His lips were dried and peeled and bloody in some places and his watery blue eyes, which Margaret Vivian had told him once resembled a beautiful large lake of pristine water, was now overflowing with the tears that he could not hold back. Margaret Vivian now sat at his bedside and watched Stanley as he valiantly fought to be strong, but this disease was too much for him and her own strength was waning. For weeks, she had watched Stanley suffer – such painful distress she thought should not, could not be borne. She tried to soothe and comfort him by feeding him cool glasses of water, but soon, he could not stomach even this and regurgitated the liquid all over herself and the clean sheets. The incident reminded her of the time, only two and one half years ago, when she had discovered his well kept secret. Even now, she did not blame him for not telling her. Even now, she did not think of her own fate. Her entire body and mind was focused on relieving Stanley of his pain, to free him from the chains of suffering and torment that was too much for one person to bear.

Margaret Vivian sat on her rocking chair next to Stanley's bed looking through the large window of the small wooden house that he had helped build in the middle of the forest. It was raining. The view from the window was extraordinary: The world in all its beauteousness spilled its abundance all over the mountains; the colours, red and blue and green and white and yellow and violet and purple, the kaleidoscope of colours, reminded her of her own vitality. She marveled that after all *those* years of pain as a child, it was in this place, she had found peace - in the same space. The beauty of nature brought to her tired spirit the focus and consistency that she had lacked in her youth. It was in the presence of nature that she was able to come to terms with her own demons - and it was so because of Stanley. He remained her bedrock, her mate, her husband, her angel. And as she rocked back and forth, back and forth, back and forth, she knew that she was tired of watching him suffer.

Margaret Vivian rocked quietly in her chair for a long, long time. Then, deliberately she raised herself off her rocking chair. Going outside, behind her scented garden, she searched for the plants that her grandmother Vivian had told her about. Vivian knew which plants were good medicine, for coughs and colds, which helped put irritable babies to sleep, which ones helped to relieve "women's problems" and which could sedate the pain of arthritis or asthma or miscarriages. As she walked in between the unruly bushes, she hoped and prayed that if there was a God that he will forgive her for what she was going to do. As she chose her herbs, she slowly wiped the dew off the leaves with the hem of her dress. Carefully, she removed the wild roots and then took the bundle of herbs into the kitchen.

She fed it to him slowly. He could not swallow much because his throat hurt too much. She could see his Adam's apple moving up and down, up and down, up and down as he tried to please her by drinking the liquid. It looked like blood, and much of the liquid ran down the side of Stanley's mouth – in the same way that it had flowed down onto the bare feet of the statue of the Virgin Mary in the convent's chapel. She turned her face away from the flow and concentrated instead on making sure that he had drunk enough. When she was finished, she placed the small glass on the bedside table. Stanley looked up at Margaret Vivian and his watery eyes were dry. He did not smile, but his eyes looked grateful. Then they seemed to focus on something or someone behind her. Margaret Vivian turned around and saw her mother watching her.

Viola stood stock still near the foot of Stanley's bed. Not a muscle moved in her body or in her face. Only her big, black eyes – so much like Margaret Vivian's - were opened wide. She stared at her child and Margaret Vivian stared back. Their eyes were locked for what seemed to be an eternity. Then, Viola looked down at the peaceful Stanley who lay on his bed with a small smile evident on his lips. He was so thin. All the bones in his face were apparent. His forehead was rounded and clearly marked. His nostrils were wide open and so was his mouth. He looked so vulnerable, but somehow peaceful. Tearing her eyes away from the man whom she had grown to admire and trust, in spite of the circumstances under which she knew him, she turned her gaze to the small glass on the bedside table. Then without a word, she turned and walked out of the room.

Viola never glanced back once, but she knew that Margaret Vivian was standing at the side of Stanley's bed, her long gangly arms hanging loosely at her side. Her large black eyes followed her mother out of the room, across the living space and into the kitchen where she disappeared down the wooden steps. Viola held on to the banister as she slowly made her way outside. Her knees were giving her a lot of pain lately, but somehow that soreness in her tired legs could not, did not match the ache in her throbbing heart. As she reached to the bottom of the stairs, she paused for a few moments to catch her breath. It was a beautiful morning. She could smell the herbs from the herb garden that Vivian and Stanley tendered so carefully. The thyme, parsley, oregano, lemon grass, mint, were all laid out in ordered rows with small paths of pebbles in between so that they were easily accessible and there was no chance of trampling the young plants. She thought to herself that this small garden was the only ordered space in Margaret Vivian's life – beside Stanley. Viola raised her nose into the air and breathed in the scents of nature mixed with the breathtaking aroma of the herbs. It had been raining the night before and the earth smelled wonderful; of dirt and moss and fresh growing things. Treading her way to the back of the house and through the large plants that made up her daughter's wild, overgrown garden, she made her way into the forest.

With the return of Margaret Vivian, Viola had returned to her beloved forest and like Margaret Vivian, it was where she found peace and tranquility – although it was somewhat different from the comforts it had afforded her in her youth. At this time in her life, the forest represented to her a different perspective; it was more a manifestation of a greater Presence and she remembered her mother's morning affirmation:

I remember the days of old,
I think about all your deeds,
I meditate on the works of your hands

As Viola lowered her body heavily onto the bank of the stream, she was thinking of Margaret Vivian and what she had just done. The "works of [Margaret Vivian's] hands" was not something that she could comprehend. Her deed was evil, vile; to be abhorred. It could not be tolerated by her, Viola. It was a fearful act and one to be condemned. Viola always knew that she did not and could not understand the workings of Margaret Vivian's mind, but this time she thought the girl had gone too far. This was really beyond limits. As she traced her long fingers in the cool, morning stream; back and forth, back and forth, back and forth she tried to recollect her thoughts ...

What Viola could not fathom was Margaret Vivian's act: Was it a sign of strength or of weakness? In spite of his treachery towards her by not admitting to his illness, Stanley and Margaret Vivian lived and cared for each other in a way that was alien to Viola's nature. She thought of Graham, her own husband, and his transgression towards her. She was not able to forgive him. She would *never* be able to forgive him. She thought that maybe, she did not have the strength to do so, so her world had collapsed into somnolence and silence. But Margaret Vivian had acted. However, did she have the moral right to commit such an act? So much arrogance was beyond Viola's comprehension. And she could not let it rest.

Viola turned back towards Margaret Vivian's small house. She needed to say something to her. She was compelled to let Margaret Vivian know that what she had done was abominable. The girl should know that you cannot take a life, since you cannot give life. But halfway there, she paused. She did not want Margaret Vivian to admit a truth that she already knew. Her courage failed her and she walked past the small house and on to her own.

Viola went into the kitchen and put the kettle on. Then, feeling that she needed some human comfort, she looked into her grand daughter's room. Olivia was reading and as usual, she was sprawled across her bed, her dress raised way above her knees. Viola lowered her body onto the bed, next to the child and pulled Olivia's dress down. Olivia looked up from her reading and was astonished to see the unhappiness on her grandmother's face. Quickly, she placed her book on the floor and sat up, close to Viola:

"What's wrong Gran, What's the matter?"

Viola did not answer. She was staring at the child, but she was not seeing her. She was remembering Margaret Vivian at this same age, reading in this same room as Olivia. Viola recalled the strength of character in the small face of the young Margaret Vivian. She recollected her stubborn streak; the force of her personality hit you every time - like a slap in the face. Viola did not understand, could not comprehend the child whom she had borne. She was not like her sister or the young girl looking up at her now with the same big black eyes as herself and as Margaret Vivian. Olivia was in every sense, the daughter of Josephine, who had been so easy to live with, so accommodating, so amenable.

However, in spite of Margaret Vivian's many offenses, her failings, her excesses, her traumatic beginning, Viola loved her best and it was this knowledge and the accompanying guilt at preference that had initiated the ambivalence in her attitude towards her. The expression of her love for Margaret Vivian went back and forth, back and forth, back and forth, from an overwhelming love and unintended admiration of her strength to a heavy dislike – even revulsion - to her excessive nature.

Her mind in turmoil and with no one else to whom she could relate the unspeakable act that Margaret Vivian had committed, Viola unburdened her troubles and her anxieties to the twelve year old Olivia and Olivia, listened in consternation to a story that she should not have been told and could not really understand. How could a young girl, not yet a teenager who loved her grandmother with all her heart and soul, comprehend the destructive love that was shared between Margaret Vivian and Viola? How could she fathom the depths of her grandmother's predicament? How could she understand the machinations of a mind as complicated as that of her Tante Margaret?

Margaret Vivian buried Stanley near the place that he had loved best, under the large chenette, tree, very close to the stream. It was an undergrowth, quite deep in the forest and although the authorities had at first resisted the request for burial there, mainly because of the rumours of what had killed Stanley, they relented after their uneasiness in the presence of the audacious Margaret Vivian got the better of them. So after some very successful coercion, they convinced themselves that they needed to rid the community, quickly, of the remains of such a disease.

It was a beautiful peaceful spot and usually, if Margaret Vivian cut some of the wide branches off her largest mango tree, she could see the chenette tree from the large window of the bedroom she had shared with Stanley.

TEN

Margaret Vivian and Olivia

Don't be afraid to go out on a limb.
That's where the fruit is.

H. JACKSON BROWNE

$\mathcal{TEN}$

$\mathcal{The}$ years passed slowly for Margaret Vivian. She spent much of her time as she had done as a child, curled up in the large chenette tree. When she stayed there – sometimes for a few days if the weather was good – she felt close to Stanley. Sometimes, she looked after her herb garden and her flower garden, both of which flourished magnificently under her care. Other times, she weeded the ferociously growing bushes around her house and planted tree after tree after tree – until the house appeared to be ensconced in a valley of foliage. Everything that Margaret Vivian ever planted grew. It was like that since she was a child and Viola, her mother, had stated to Olivia that that particular gift was the first thing that had attracted her to her grandfather, Graham.

Olivia, Margaret Vivian's niece, who, at first seemed terrified of her, now accepted her presence around her grandmother's house, for Viola and Margaret Vivian still visited each other – although the visits were not as frequent as they used to be before Stanley's death. Since the death of Stanley, Viola was wont to stay away from Margaret Vivian and although they were civil to each other, they had lost that vital connection that had helped recharge their relationship.

Olivia, who called her aunt Tante Margaret, became immensely attracted to the increasingly eccentric Margaret Vivian, but at the same time she felt an aversion to her. Olivia spent hours looking at Margaret Vivian as she kept her garden. She peeped at her from behind trees as she washed her clothes in the stream and she stared openly at her when she came by to look for Viola. Margaret Vivian sensed that the child was afraid of her. This fear of Margaret Vivian had its root in the teachings of Viola who trained the girl to believe in the very circumscribed roles of women. As a result, Olivia's concept of womanhood and femaleness was locked into two roles; that of wife or mother. Viola was incapable of introducing Olivia to any other meaningful roles. So that the revolutionary, unprecedented presence of Margaret Vivian in their small, closed, insular village was the first time that Olivia – and for that matter any of Olivia's friends - had seen any female who was able to forage within herself and find 'other' identities, particularly those of individual thinker or lover - and who used her mouth, that is, her words as a powerful weapon. So to Olivia, her Tante Margaret was someone of whom she was afraid - and at the same time, ashamed. In the village, it was whispered that Margaret Vivian had sucked all the emotion and all the energy for life out of her old, tired mother. They said she had devoured the life of her lover and did not like children. Consequently, Olivia was surprised and curious about this woman who not only lived on the edge of their small village but who exhibited no concern for the villagers or their children. To Olivia the horrendous act her grandmother had confided that she had committed against her Uncle Stanley revealed that Tante Margaret was evil. Even her grandmother had told her that Margaret Vivian was the devil incarnate.

It was during this time, in her late teenage years, when Olivia was attempting to find herself that her grandmother, Margaret Vivian's mother died. It was early one rainy Wednesday morning and Viola had gotten up early to feed the chickens, as usual. Her oldest son, Mark, who tended the farm, had gone to the beach to buy fish. Viola, after having her morning coffee, sat in the cool of the verandah. She did not feel well and decided to take a nap until Mark returned and it was time to wake Olivia to go to school.

It was eight o'clock when Olivia stirred in her bed. She was always a late riser and had to be cajoled out of her bed in order not to be late for school. The rays of the early morning sun slanted across her bed and the heat of it awakened her. Stretching lazily, she wondered where her grandmother was and why did she not wake her. She enjoyed her grandmother's wake up call. Usually she will sing her morning welcome and tickle her under her feet, a sensation she particularly enjoyed. Olivia padded barefoot out to the kitchen, but her grandmother was not there. She called to her from the verandah as she thought she may have been outside near the hen house but there was no response. Sensing some catastrophe, she ran back into the house and entered her grandmother's bedroom calling loudly;

"Granma Ma, Ma Ma! Where are you? What's wrong?"

As she entered the room, she saw her grandmother lying very still on her bed. More to relieve her own anxiety than to be playful, she tickled her under her feet but there was no response. Olivia was frightened. She shook Viola by her shoulders and as she did so, Viola's head fell to one side and rolled off the pillow. Olivia sprang back from the bed and her voice rose to a crescendo;

"Ma Ma!! Ma Ma!! Ma Ma!!"

Then Olivia began to scream. Margaret Vivian, far out, working in her herb garden heard the shrill noise and stood still to listen for a moment. Then she heard the noise again and recognized the high-pitched sound as Olivia's voice. Dropping the small tool with which she was cutting the wild growth off her lemon grass, she began to run towards her mother's house and then she saw Olivia flying along the sand path calling her name;

"Tante Margaret! Tante Margaret!"

Margaret Vivian caught hold of the girl and she collapsed onto the ground screaming that she could not wake up her grandmother. Quieting her for a moment, Margaret Vivian led the hysterical girl back to her mother's house and led her up the wooden steps. Olivia, frightened and overcome with emotion, refused to enter her grandmother's bedroom so she sat at the edge of one of the wooden chairs in the living room making small keening noises. Therefore, it was Margaret Vivian alone, who entered her mother's bedroom.

The bed was freshly made and Viola was lying sideways on the yellow bedspread in her pink morning shift. One leg – her right leg - was bent under the other. Her head was off the pillow and there was some white fluid at one corner of her mouth. Her right hand was lying over her left breast and her left hand, was underside. Even before getting close to the bed, Margaret Vivian knew that Viola was dead. She stood still near the door for a while and looked at her mother. Viola looked tired. Her brow was furrowed and her eyes were half closed. Margaret Vivian felt a deep pain in the pit of her stomach. She tried to move closer to the bed, but her legs were heavy; they did not obey her command so she let herself fall slowly down onto her mother's old rocking chair. She sat there, very quiet for a moment and then slowly, she began to rock; back and forth, back and forth, back and forth. The movement of the rocking chair increased - quickly, incessantly - until suddenly, coming to her senses, she abruptly stopped rocking. Then, she raised her eyes to her mother's form and in one lingering look, gazed at her from head to toe: from the top of head where her hair was in a tight bun to the brown underside of her left foot. She then brought her hands together on her lap, the fingers intertwined. And for the first time in her entire life Margaret Vivian cried. The tears flowed down her face and onto her breast. She did not make a sound. She made no effort to wipe the tears away. Then she got up from her mother's rocking chair, walked across to her bed and wiped the white liquid away from her mother's mouth with the hem of her dress. With a small prayer – from where it came, she did not know - she closed her mother's eyes.

Her mother had died without ever uttering a word to her about Stanley's death.

Then remembering that the child Olivia would need her attention, she walked into the living room and sat next to her. She did not touch her, for she did not wish to frighten her further. Olivia looked at her aunt and her big black eyes were open wide and wild. Then, Margaret Vivian placed her long arms around the girl, her sister's child, and thought that she was so much like her mother, Josephine. She knew she had to look after her. Margaret Vivian then said to herself that the girl needed to go away from SouthWood so she could find herself; become independent and self reliant. She thought she could do this for her sister since she had nothing to do with all that money Stanley had left.

ELEVEN

Margaret Vivian

I feel like one who has done work for the day to retire awhile,
I receive now again of my many translations, from my avataras ascending,
while others doubtless await me,
An unknown sphere more real than I dream'd, more direct, darts
awakening rays about me, So long!
Remember my words, I may again return,
I love you, I depart from materials,
I am as one disembodied, triumphant, dead.

Walt Whitman, <u>Leaves of Grass</u>

ELEVEN

It was only a week after viola's funeral and the house where she had lived her entire life was quiet. Olivia sat on the wooden steps with the house pet in her lap. She played with the dog's ear and he in turn, turned around to lick her face. Olivia wiped away the wetness with the back of her hand and then dried her hand on her skirt. Margaret Vivian was sitting on Viola's rocking chair on the verandah. She had begun making plans for the girl to leave the small village. She thought that Olivia could stay for a short while with Sister Sarah Rose at her old convent school and then she would travel to the Unites States to finish school. She was to stay with her uncle and aunt in New York.

The visitors came every night and the brothers, Mark and Thomas and their old friends hosted them every night as was the custom – until forty nights had passed. The nightly vigil was a trial for Margaret Vivian, who was tired of the large crowds. She was also intolerant of their invasive and persistent curiosity about her. On many nights, she ran away to her own haven in the forest and slept there. She felt at peace there. In addition, she had begun to feel very, very tired and had lost much weight which she had at first attributed to the passing of her mother.

But the loss of weight was relentless, so much so that she had begun to think seriously of her own illness, her own death maybe from the disease that had taken Stanley away from her. At first she was afraid – for a short while - and then she remembered reading C.S. Lewis on her return to university. He had written:

No one ever told me that grief felt so like fear.

She contemplated. The quote brought immediately and forcefully to her mind the fact that everyone she truly loved had departed this life: Stanley had left her many years and now, her mother, with whom she had such a destructive relationship, but on whom she now knew she had depended upon for emotional sustenance, had also died. She was alone in the world and somehow her garden, the river, the trees, the sunlight, the seas, did not seem to nourish her spirit as much as they used to. So valiantly Margaret Vivian said to herself, death, where is *your* sting? For Margaret Vivian there was no *sting*. She realized that the pain and hurt she experienced came because of separation from the two people she had loved most; Stanley and her mother. Reconciling herself to her fate, Margaret Vivian went into her mother's house, took her old rocking chair from her bedroom and brought it to her haven in the forest. She had decided that she would sit and wait on death. She would rock herself to sleep - for comfort - until the 'long sleep': back and forth, back and forth, back and forth.

I have desired and gazed into the distance too long . I have belonged to solitude too long: thus I have forgotten how to be silent.

I have become nothing but speech and the tumbling of a brook from high rocks: I want to hurl my words down into the valleys.

And let my stream of love plunge into impassable and pathless places!

How should a stream not find its way to the sea at last

Nietzsche!

Margaret Vivian's wait was long and painful. For five years she waited. Slowly, her health declined and she came to depend on her old and only Uncle Mark, who cared for her as well as she did for his mother. He was helped by one of the village women Miss Esther, who was not afraid of this frightening disease or its terrifying manifestation of physical disintegration. Miss Esther cared for the sick and suffering Margaret Vivian as best as she could, but she too was old – as old as her Uncle Mark.

On Olivia's first trip back home from the United States, she was overcome by the deterioration in her aunt's health. However, she returned to her studies in the New York, in a good frame of mind, after Margaret Vivian had consoled her that she would be alright. Her uncle and Miss Esther would look after her and she was in the best place that she could be; in the forest, in her home, close to Stanley.

However, on Olivia's second visit, nine months later, she was confronted with the disintegration and collapse of her aunt's mental as well as physical state. Ms. Esther had died and Uncle Mark could not cope. The family had sent for Olivia.

Now, Olivia stood near to her bed and did not know what to do...

TWELVE

Caged birds accept each other but flight is what they long for.

Tennessee Williams

TWELVE

Margaret Vivian felt a sudden whooshing sensation and her body seem to plummet into the depths of a deep, dark tomb... The darkness was overwhelming. It seemed to envelop her, pushing her down, down, down into some bottomless pit. Suddenly, the whole space was transformed. But Margaret Vivian was not afraid ... there was no time to be afraid. She seemed to have been catapulted into a place where to be there was to experience, in vivid colour, a world she had not known but had longed for her entire life. It was as if she was flung into this compensatory dream-world in which all the feelings of want and lack she had suffered before were eclipsed by a rapture in which form and feeling, where object; tree and rock and stream were clearly visible and where everything she perceived was lucid and very pleasurable. All the conflicts and trauma she had experienced in the 'dead zone'- between birth and death - were eliminated, completely extinguished. It was breathtaking. Suddenly, she felt her body lift upwards. It seemed to accelerate, moving quickly towards a white light that resembled the radiance of the breaking of dawn in her early childhood. There, the sun had slanted into her bedroom window and the warmth of the morning sun had wrapped her and her rocking chair in a comforting gentle glow. As she thought about this image, it materialized. Her own rocking chair! But this time, the chair seemed newly polished and she noticed that there was no dust in its crevices. She thought to herself, 'that's not my rocking chair! My chair was always full with dirty garments hanging from its every limb". This rocking chair seemed to have become a part and a point in a large painting. In its composition, the chair was both focus and form. The chair held her attention for a long time. It was significant. It seemed to come alive: It rocked back and forth, back and forth, back and forth. She became excited on seeing it. She felt at peace by its movement, was enthralled by its shape. The rocking chair became at the same time not only something that had function, but as she stared at it, it seemed to be filled with vitality as it rocked back and forth, back and forth, back and forth in a systematic fashion that gave it, its form, its beauty. She could smell the teak out of which it was made; the beautiful carvings on the arms reminded her of the art of Michelangelo in the cathedral in Rome. To behold it was a pleasure.

Remembering how important rocking chairs were in her life rendered the experience of looking at it extraordinary: It was the last chair her father had sat on. She remembered sitting on one at her father's wake. She recollected Josephine hiding behind one on her father's death. She too, had fallen into one on realizing that her mother was dead. She recalled that when she had given up her soul to her fate, after Stanley's death, she was sitting on one. It was in that same chair – or one like it - that she had been rocked as a child, the same in which Josephine, her sister, had rocked her child, Olivia. Passing beyond this image, Margaret Vivian floated upwards serenely and saw herself, watching, as her body, now clothed in a red flowing garment, moved past her, like lightning, very much like her uncle's 'marabunta' kite, moving and undulating in the hot midday sun in their village on Sunday afternoons. She was lifted again and was swirled around in a refreshing breeze. She thought to herself – where did this breeze come from? It felt cool on her skin, like the blue waters of the river at home, but although this movement of air appeared to be light, it was able to lift her body upwards, upwards, towards what? And then she saw her mother. Viola was as big as Life. She was standing ahead of Margaret Vivian – in the light. Her arms were stretched out towards her. A long flowing green garment swathed her body and her head was covered with a white cloth. The green garment swirled around her as she moved and only her big black eyes were visible - and her mouth. She looked like a tree: Stalwart and tall. It occurred to Margaret Vivian then, that maybe, maybe, her mother was, for her, the Tree of Life. She had spread herself outwards and upwards to embrace all; children, husband, mother, grandchild. But maybe, she had spread herself too thin; too much to do, too many to serve. As a consequence she had known no one: not her husband, not her children – not even herself, and certainly not Margaret Vivian. And because of this lack of knowledge, Viola was forced into silence: words could not be said - because she could not express what she did not know Meeting her mother in this celestial space allowed Margaret Vivian to understand that the fusion of intellect, as what is known and understood in reality, and spirit; as what is unknown, but expressed through strength, courage, determination and heart, are the qualities that can lead to knowledge. Through this sudden illumination, Margaret Vivian acquired insight into her life and that of her mother's. Knowledge about her mother was not available to her before. However, now in this surreal space, she recognized that her mother had given of herself as freely as she could, never expecting anything in return. Like a tree which fruit is in great abundance, which proffers its fruit unconditionally, much had fallen and rotted on the earth at its feet; delectable, but untasted, uneaten, unenjoyed. In this state of enlightenment, she was freed from worldly ties and physical entanglements, freed from emotional suffering which had been her living reality. Now, because of this knowledge and understanding, Margaret Vivian was able to go where she will – soar where she wont. She had entered a realm where the search for Truth was possible. Crossing the threshold of reality, Margaret Vivian had been catapulted into the realm of the Imagination, into a mythical space where memory of her mother buttressed her and where this remembrance kept the fire of imagination burning in her long suffering heart[h]. In truth, Viola's presence – as memory- and the fire of Margaret Vivian's own imagination had given her access to a place where reality and memory coalesce, creating a space in which she could be at home. Thus, Margaret Vivian, while laying prostrate on her untidy bed – alone and unafraid - came to her final conclusion : that, in reality, one's place in an extraordinary world can rest on the fusion of Memory and Imagination, created through a realisation that in relationships one can find Ultimate Truth.

In the end, after it was finished, all Olivia, daughter of her sister Josephine had to do, was to close Margaret Vivian's half-opened eyes - so that she could see clearly:

As our circle of knowledge expands, so does the circumference of darkness surrounding it. ...

Imagination is more important than knowledge.

Albert Einstein